My Blue Lady

Middlemarch Shifters 14

Shelley Munro

My Blue Lady

Print ISBN: 978-1-99-106317-5
Digital ISBN: 978-0-9951026-4-4

Editor: Mary Moran

Cover: Kim Killion, The Killion Group

Munro Press, New Zealand.

First Munro Press electronic publication September 2017

First Munro Press print publication February 2023

For Paul.

Introduction

Saber and Emily Mitchell have been mates for years and happy until the tragic loss of their baby changes everything.

Feline shapeshifter, Saber is having a tough week with family and community problems. Worse, his beloved Emily has shut him out and is wallowing in depression. They inhabit the same house, but his loving mate has withdrawn. It's time to up the ante because the growing rift is driving him to despair. Armed with a bag of sex toys and a tropical island setting, Saber is determined to seduce his mate to his way of thinking, to drive the blues away, and he won't take no for an answer.

CHAPTER ONE

SABER MITCHELL SAT IN the crowded courtroom, every muscle in his body quivering, demanding action. He fought his feline self, his human self, and gripped his mate's hand as an anchor. Emily sat at his side, silent and unmoving, face pale and drawn. His gaze sought Sly, his younger brother who stood accused in the dock.

Sly focused on the wall at the far end of the room, eyes never deviating from the spot he'd chosen for his attention. His expression remained stoic, as it had throughout the trial. His attitude hadn't gained approval from the jury. His lawyer hadn't bothered calling him to the stand, the evidence against Sly overwhelming.

This would not end well.

The jury filed back into the court and took their seats. Whispers sped around the gallery, earning glares from the court officials. Seated on his other side, Joe, Sly's twin, practically vibrated with tension. Saber reached for his hand, hoping to stay any impulsive acts on Joe's part.

No one, apart from Sly, Joe, and their accuser Maggie Scarlet knew what had happened that day. Sly and Joe insisted Maggie was lying to save her skin. Joe had wanted to tell the cops everything, that he'd been present too, but Sly had refused the offer. He'd said Maggie's high-priced lawyers and her convincing lies would have them both in jail. One brother accused was bad enough. Saber agreed and had backed Sly.

No sense dragging in both twins when the cops didn't realize Joe's part in the alleged crime. Maggie had kept quiet, which raised questions in Saber's mind. The answers added together and spelled selfish bitch. Saber kicked his rush of anger to the curb, covering it with an icy control that allowed him to function.

The jury settled, taking their seats. The judge leaned forward and peered at them over the top of his glasses. "Have you reached a decision?"

The foreman stood. "Yes, your honor."

"How do you find the defendant on the charges of abduction and abuse?"

"We find the defendant guilty."

The gallery, filled with their friends and family, erupted into protest. The judge bashed on the desk with his gavel.

"Order in the court," one of the officials shouted.

Sullen silence fell, and as the judge delivered the sentence, Sly's gaze shifted to Saber before flitting to Joe. In that brief glimpse, Saber caught his brother's anguish before resignation slid into place and closed off his emotions.

Saber listened to the judge, heart pounding, feline snarling silently for release. Beside him, Joe twitched and Saber tightened his grip to the point of pain. A silent order to maintain control.

"I sentence you to ten years imprisonment," the judge intoned.

Saber shot to his feet, helplessness engulfing him. A lump clogged his throat as a court employee led Sly away. Joe and Emily stood beside him, both silent, both shocked. Sid and the rest of the Feline council had urged him to think ahead, to make plans to keep Sly safe within the prison environment. *Just in case.* Now, he was glad he'd listened to them. His plans would ensure no one discovered Sly's feline genes during standard medical tests. The rest was up to Sly. Somehow, his brother had to battle his feline side and retain his human form.

Hell, what a bloody mess. Saber blinked rapidly, swallowed twice, and sucked in a deep breath before straightening his shoulders.

"Let's go," he said gruffly.

Over an hour later, he dropped Joe at the twins' farmhouse.

"Are you going to be all right?"

"No," Joe bit off. "My brother is in jail, and the charges are bullshit."

Saber cut him some slack since he wanted to lash out as well. "Do you want me to arrange for someone to stay with you?"

"I want to be alone."

Saber nodded. "All right. I'll check with you in the morning. If you need anything, any help on your farm, ring me. I'm sure Felix or Leo would be glad to lend a hand."

Joe gave a terse nod. "I-I... Not right now, Saber."

Saber got it. Joe needed to shore up his defenses alone. He shot a quick glance at Emily. Her brown hair, longer than normal and devoid of the golden highlights she used to love, hid her face. But he could guess her expression without seeing her. Her brown eyes would look reddened and exhausted, her grief digging lines into her forehead.

She hadn't said a word on the way home. Losing their baby had hit them hard, and she'd retreated into herself. This quietness wasn't new. He sighed. "I'll see you tomorrow."

Once the lights turned on in the twins' house, Saber backed from the drive and headed home.

"Do you think Maggie will change her story and tell the truth?"

Emily started. "What?"

Saber struggled with his temper and silently counted to three before he repeated his question.

"No."

"No?"

"Too much to lose," Emily said.

"So she'd send an innocent man to jail rather than tell the truth?"

"Yes."

That was his reading of the woman too. *A self-centered bitch.* Saber pressed his lips together to corral the harsh

7

words pushing for release. He was lucky his mate was speaking to him at all. Emily was hurting. He understood that, but dammit, he'd lost a baby too. "I'm going for a run."

Emily looked at him this time, her eyes wide in the dim light of the car interior. "How long will you be?"

Saber parked in their driveway and switched off the ignition. "I have no idea," he snapped. He held a lot of anger pulsing for release. The way he felt right now he could run all night and barely scratch the surface.

She frowned a fraction then nodded.

"I'll come inside first. I want to ring Gavin and check that his friend saw Sly."

Emily picked up her handbag and exited the car without another word. Her heels clicked on the footpath as she headed for the front door. Saber stared after her in frustration. It felt as if she was punishing him for the loss of their baby. He hit his head on the steering wheel twice before he followed his wife inside.

He strode for his office and rang Gavin, the local vet and feline doctor. "It's Saber," he said when Gavin answered. "Did your friend see Sly?"

"Yes," Gavin said. "I spoke with him ten minutes ago. Sly is safe. No one will guess he's a feline shifter."

"Now all Sly has to do is survive the rest of the inmates."

"I'm so sorry, Saber."

Saber smothered a yawn. "Not your fault. There was nothing any of us could do. I'll see you at the meeting tomorrow night."

"Care to give me a hint what it's about?"

"You'll hear tomorrow. Don't forget to bring Charlie. All human mates must attend as well as our shifter population."

"Now I'm curious," Gavin said with a laugh.

"Tomorrow," Saber said and hung up. "Emily, I'm going now." He gave an irritable shrug on hearing silence. This yawning gap between them was killing him. He had to do something and soon before their marriage imploded beyond the point of no return. But first...first he'd run off his temper and frustration and mentally prepare for the rest of the week.

Saber stripped at the door and shifted, embracing the discomfort as bones and muscles reshaped to feline. Then, he was off.

The fresh air sawed in and out of his lungs as he raced down the drive and across paddocks, dodging rocks and a fallen tree stump. He took the fence without slowing, the exertion doing nothing to quell his writhing fury. He wanted—needed—to hit someone. *Something*.

His fury, his aggravation, his anxiety didn't shift, so he kept running and running and running, attempting to outrace his thoughts. His muscles rippled with each long stride, his breathing heavier than when he had started this madcap race.

The rumble of a vehicle slowed his unrelenting pace, and he slid into the shadows. The last thing he wanted was for a human to see him and report their sighting to the authorities or worse, the media. Given the subject matter of the feline community meeting tomorrow night that would be a catastrophe. He issued a throaty grunt and resumed his run once the utility vehicle roared away from Middlemarch.

On the outskirts of the town, he paused. He hadn't meant to run so far. Drunken laughter reached him, but not from the pub as he'd expect. Curiosity aroused, he slunk through the shadows, heading toward the racket. His nostrils twitched as he inhaled, every sense working to provide clues. Paint? Manure? More drunken laughter ensued, then the revving of a vehicle.

As Saber crept around the corner of the co-op store to peer through the darkness and the brighter light cast from a flickering streetlight, the SUV sped off. The rest of the main street appeared empty and after double-checking to make certain, Saber prowled to the front of the co-op store.

The drunken idiots had done a real job on the frontage of the building. Mud—no, his sense of smell confirmed manure—splattered the window along with crooked words in white paint.

Leave town. Not wanted. No mixed marriages.

Saber glared at the messages. Those felines—including him—who'd married humans were richer for the experience. The humans who knew about feline shapeshifters had contributed to the community and continued to do so. They were no danger to the feline population, but these idiots were like a ticking clock attached to a bomb.

With another glance to ensure he wasn't observed, he prowled the length of the town. The co-op wasn't the only building trashed. They'd vandalized Patels' supermarket, Emily's café, Storm in a Teacup, and the new bank. The school hall and the area where the weekly market took place. Saber did a circuit of the back streets and scowled at the police station. Cow shit and slogans in white paint covered the steps and the front door.

Saber let out a testy growl and followed it up with a feline hiss. This would stop before these idiots tore their community apart.

Picking up the pace, he trotted toward the vet surgery. That, at least, had escaped the graffiti and vandalism. Saber shifted and pounded on the door. He waited, listened, and thumped on the door again.

"I'm coming, dammit," a testy voice said.

The door flew open to reveal Gavin Finley. He was obviously straight out of bed. His black hair stood on end while his expression held a serving of pissed. His face cleared on seeing Saber. "What is it? Emily? Sly?"

"No, I need Charlie. Can you ring Laura and get her to come into town too? Do you have a camera? I don't have my phone."

"Come in while I rouse Charlie."

Saber glanced down at his nakedness. "I need to stay in human form for a bit. Can I borrow a pair of sweatpants?"

Charlie McKenzie, one of the local cops, appeared in the hallway, dressed but rumpled. "Leticia said it was for me. What's happened?"

"Most of the businesses in town have been vandalized," Saber said tersely. "We need everything photographed before we start cleaning."

"I can take photos with my phone," Leticia, Charlie's and Gavin's mate, appeared beside Charlie. "I can help."

When Gavin protested, she held up a hand. "I'm awake anyway. I take it you want the evidence cleaned away before morning when unsuspecting humans awaken?"

"That's the plan," Saber said.

Gavin sighed. "I'm awake now too. Saber, I'll grab you clothes and come to help."

"Laura and Jonno are on their way," Charlie said. "Henry and Gerard will help. The Patel crew too."

Saber nodded. "I'd prefer not to spend the entire night scrubbing. The important thing is that we photograph each building before we start cleaning. I want evidence to present to the meeting tomorrow night. I want to confront the culprits and inform them of the consequences should they repeat this little prank."

Charlie straightened from his slouch. "You know who did it?"

"I do," Saber said in a hard voice. "And I'm in just the mood to knock a few heads together."

Spending the entire night scouring off graffiti did little to improve Saber's mood. London Allbright, a human and a member of the Feline council, had promised to collect together the damming photos and make them into a movie to show at the meeting. He hadn't decided on a course of action yet, but he had the rest of the day to think.

"See you tonight," Charlie said as he pulled up outside Saber's house, just after six.

"Tell Gavin I'll replace his sweatpants for him," Saber said, grateful for the ride home. At this time of the year, it was light in the mornings and he hadn't wanted to risk someone seeing him in his feline form.

"He keeps spare pairs in case his patients need them," Charlie said.

"Thanks for helping," Saber replied.

Charlie shrugged. "All part of the job."

Emily sat at the kitchen counter, her hands cupped around a mug of coffee. "Where have you been?"

Saber bit back the retort tickling his throat. The truth—given her current state of mind, he didn't think she'd care. Instead, he opened the cupboard and pulled out a mug. He filled it with coffee before he turned to answer. "There was a problem in town."

"A woman problem?"

"What? No!" Saber gaped at Emily, shocked at the implication, that she'd think he'd cheat on her. He'd never. Emily was his mate. "I've been with Charlie, Laura, Jonno, and Gavin," he said. "I don't want to tell you why, but you'll learn more at the meeting tonight."

Emily's gaze avoided his and her shoulders hunched. He thought she believed him. Maybe he should reiterate his position.

"Emily, you are my mate. I love you."

She glanced at him briefly then, her brown eyes glossy with tears. She set down her mug with a thump and slid off her barstool. "I'd better go and shower. I promised London I'd help with the early morning baking at the café."

Saber stared at her departing back. "Crap." He didn't know what to do, was at a loss as to how to fix their marriage. Something had to change...

CHAPTER TWO

VEHICLES RANGING FROM FARM-DIRTY to city-glossy filled the paddock at the end of the private road. The hayshed, kept especially for feline community meetings, hummed with conversation.

Saber strolled to the doorway where Agnes Paisley and Valerie McClintock, members of the Feline council, ticked off names of the family members as they arrived. A glimpse inside the barn showed Brian, Agnes's son, had arranged the seating and pulled out the raised platform they used for a stage. Gerard and Henry had hooked up the sound system and arranged a video screen as he'd requested.

"Is everyone here?" Saber asked, his mind only half on the question as he watched Emily attempt a smile for her sisters-in-law. She failed, and it was easy for him to see their concern, although they hid it in warm embraces and bright laughter. He forced away his dejection and worry to concentrate on the coming evening.

Valerie pushed her glasses up her nose and lifted her head. "Surprisingly, yes."

Agnes gave a pleased nod, the corners of her mouth lifting to ease her normal stern frown. "All shifters and human mates accounted for. I thought we'd need to track people down."

"A few of our lot will wish they'd stayed away by the time I finish with them," Saber said, his tone grim.

"Don't blow it, lad," Valerie ordered.

"Since I have a human mate, Sid will handle the formalities. This meeting is too important to our community. We don't want an element of our population saying I'm laying down the law to accommodate my human mate."

Agnes's querulous expression popped into prominence. "Emily is an important part of our town. No one will say that, Saber."

Saber sighed. "Not true. You'll see."

Sid climbed onto the makeshift stage and the din of conversations reduced. The locals took this as a sign to take their seats. Saber ushered Agnes and Valerie closer to Sid and once they took seats next to Ben, he settled beside London.

Sid lifted his right hand and silence fell. "We have called this meeting for all feline and wolf residents plus their human mates because we have become aware of a sector of our community who believe it is wrong for us to mate with humans. No, wait," Sid called against the burst of voices. "Let me finish my piece, then you can stand and state your opinions. Not so long ago, we were a population of farmers. The younger felines were mostly male and had no hope of finding mates if they decided to stay and work the land. The Feline council at the time, which included me, decided the only way to help our population prosper was to organize a dance to bring women of marriageable age into our community. We hoped that some of the women would be compatible and open-minded enough to accept our feline shifter status. Our first success came when Saber Mitchell met then mated with Emily.

"Since the first dance, many of our young men have settled with humans. We've added to our community by welcoming tiger and lion shifters and more recently werewolves. Middlemarch is prospering. We have new businesses, the most recent addition is a branch of Kiwi Bank, which has made life much easier for our residents and attracts visitors from other nearby towns to do their banking. Our weekly markets are popular while the youngsters have more to do during their leisure time. We've organized a Zombie Run, a rugby tournament and we still have the annual dance. We have exercise and self-defense classes and other activities, many of which are run by human mates.

"So it distresses me to learn that some of our feline population are picking on the humans who are part of our community. I've heard reports of heckling and vandalism." Sid nodded at Gerard. "Start the video, lad. This is the latest attack of vandalism where hooligans targeted every Middlemarch business with human connections."

Saber watched the start of the video with everyone else and refrained from turning to stare at the perpetrators. Whispers drifted to him, some shocked while others weren't surprised at the destruction.

The movie finished with the police station where the worst slurs were plastered over the walls. *Keep the breed pure. No humans here. Felines rule. Oust all puny humans. Half-breeds abomination.*

"This meeting serves as a warning to all," Sid thundered, looking as stern and pissed as Saber had ever seen him. "Your last warning. Let me be clear. The human integration into our population has saved our town, saved our livelihoods and saved our species. Any member of our population who is found defacing buildings or property belonging to human mates or who verbally or physically abuse them in any way will be punished. I have heard this bullying has spread to our children, and I will not stand for this behavior from any member of our community, no matter what their age."

"You're making this up," a masculine voice called from the back. "I didn't see any hint of damage when I came into town this morning."

Bullshit. Saber bounded to his feet and turned to face his community. "I'm sorry you were disappointed, Charles. I witnessed you and your friends trashing the co-op shop and the other buildings around town. I spent the entire night cleaning up the mess at Storm in a Teacup."

"You expect me to believe you cleaned by yourself?" Charles Rutherford sneered. Marsh Rutherford, his son, had married a human, and Charles had done his best to destroy the marriage. He'd pushed and pushed until Marsh had decided he'd had enough and had moved with his wife and children to another district. The man was still bitter about the help Saber had given his son.

"I cleaned all night," Laura said in a hard voice. "And lack of sleep makes me mean. It's not too late to arrest you for a crime you seem to know an awful lot about."

Charlie stood and turned to face Charles Rutherford. "I lost sleep because I cleaned all night. I scrubbed the tags off the police station."

Saber watched with pride when every other volunteer stood and rattled off what they had done to contribute to the cleaning effort.

"This video was not manufactured out of thin air," Sid called. "Our team of volunteers photographed every building before they restored them to normal."

Charles sneered. "I'm allowed to have an opinion. You're all mouth and no action. What are you going to do with me? Will I go to jail like Sly Mitchell?"

Saber struggled to hold his temper, his claws sliding beyond his fingernails and his canines protruding to crowd his mouth.

"We're going to arrest you as soon as this meeting ends," Laura snapped.

"And," Sid shouted above the outbursts. "Since you've outed yourself and exhibit no remorse for your actions, we'll make an example of you. This weekend at the market, you will be chained in stocks. Anyone who wishes to participate may pelt you with eggs or rotten vegetables. If, after this punishment, you do not mend your ways, we will force you from the community. Your mate and the rest of your family may stay, but you will no longer be welcome. I don't think you realize how much you count on the support of the community. It is difficult being a shapeshifter alone with no backup. I suggest you think about this before you commit another crime." Sid surveyed his audience.

"You can't do that," Charles shouted. "You have no authority."

"Think yourself lucky that times have changed," Sid said in a mild voice. "When I was a lad, the members of the Feline council sentenced a wrongdoer to death. Feline communities in other parts of the world still utilize this punishment." His final words fell on shocked silence.

Saber's jaw tightened at Sid's announcement. He didn't endorse the death punishment and prayed Charles would back down.

When no one added to the conversation, Sid continued. "To make sure you understand the seriousness of this matter, I expect you to sign a declaration before you leave. Each member of the community from school age upward will sign their understanding of this announcement. We stand together as a community, feline, wolf and human mates. *That* is the way forward. Do I make myself clear?"

Sid raked the audience with his glower. Saber had expected pushback, yet it didn't come, not even from Charles.

"Now, for the rest of business, I'll turn this meeting over to Saber. Charles Rutherford, come outside with me now. I'd like a private discussion with you about your fellow conspirators."

Saber rose to take Sid's place on the stage. He surveyed the faces turned to him and watched Charles Rutherford stand and stomp from the hayshed. Sid ambled after him as Saber spoke about the upcoming Halloween celebration.

He kept it short before he asked for ideas and questions from the community.

"Can I tease my friend about having a boyfriend?" Sylvie Mitchell piped up. "Am I allowed to do that?"

Tomasine Mitchell popped up, standing to face her daughter. "You can tease her, but that isn't very nice of you. You won't end up locked in the stocks, but if I hear about it, you *will* scrub the kitchen floor." She placed her hands on her hips. "Do you understand?"

A ripple of laughter filled the hayshed, and Saber silently blessed his niece.

"Sylvie, if you pick on her because she is a human or get in a fistfight with a boy because he called her a stupid human, then you will receive a warning and get pelted with rotten vegetables," he said. "I suggest that if you're not sure about a course of action, you shouldn't go ahead without seeking advice from your parents or from a councilmember. In fact, that goes for everyone.

"If you have doubts or questions, please talk with a councilmember. We are here to help and serve you. None of us wishes to force laws or rules on our residents, but this is a safety matter. It keeps everyone in the shifter community safe from government attention. Which brings me to the final matter. We want everyone within our group to know what to do if a human witnesses one of us in our animal form. With that in mind, we intend to run a drill. Since this is so important, we will repeat this drill every six months. Bring your questions and suggestions next time."

The meeting broke up and family groups drifted outside.

Emily approached him, her forehead scrunched in concentration. "You spent the entire night cleaning graffiti off the café windows?"

"Yes." Plus several other buildings in town, but he kept it simple.

Emily stared at him, opened her mouth to say something and shook her head. "Thank you."

"You're welcome." In the past he would've hugged her, wrapped his arms around her and kissed her. But now, with the yawning gap between them, all casual affection had ceased and discomfort twanged in its stead. Saber cleared his throat. "I won't be long."

Emily studied him for a fraction longer before dipping her head in acceptance. She turned away, gazing neither left or right as she exited the hayshed. In the past, his mate would've chatted...

Saber shook himself from thoughts of how things used to be between them and answered questions for several friends and neighbors.

"How is Sly?" one elderly woman asked, her eyes full of nosy interest.

"I haven't visited him yet," Saber said politely when he wanted to snarl at her for her curiosity. "Oh, sorry to rush away. I must see my brother Leo before he leaves." Saber scuttled from the hayshed before someone else tried to interrogate him about the new skeleton in the Mitchell cupboard. His mouth twisted as he slowed to a stomp. How long before some of the more militant feline shapeshifters demanded he resign from the council because Sly was now a convicted criminal? And he, by association, had become tainted.

"Hey, Saber," Leo said, straightening from his lean against his SUV. "Tough week."

"Understatement," Saber replied and dragged his hand through his hair. It was long, and he needed a haircut. Emily used to remind him. He studied his younger brother. Leo came between Felix and the twins in age and, according to Emily and the other local women, had scored in the looks department. Although Leo had dressed in jeans, casual shirt and jacket, much the same as him, Saber felt older and scruffier in comparison. "I'm surprised they didn't demand I resign from the council."

"The smart ones know they'd have to replace you and that you do a lot of unpaid work for the community," Leo said. "How's Emily?"

"About the same." Saber didn't dissemble, not with his brother. "Do you think Charles and his mates will toe the line?"

"Hard to say. Could go either way. What are you going to do if they call your bluff?"

"We'll expel them from the community as promised. Truthfully, I hope it doesn't get that far because most of the culprits have familial ties in Middlemarch. I don't think they get what it's like when you're cut off from those ties."

Leo nodded. "When can we visit Sly at the prison?"

"From what I understand, Sly authorizes the people he wishes to see by sending us an application form. We complete the form, send it back to the prison for them to approve. Once that happens we have to book a visit."

"Do they search us?"

"Yes."

"Fun times," Leo said. "How is Joe?"

"Not good. We'll have to keep an eye on him."

"Okay. Isabella and I can help Joe. That's not a problem. Let me know about Sly, and if you and the council need muscle, call on Isabella." His mouth twisted in a small grin. "She'd enjoy knocking a few heads together."

"I'll keep that in mind," Saber said dryly.

Sid came rushing up with Ben at his heels. "Good, you're still here, Saber. Charles has gone. Says he's not going to stay in this hick town with our outdated ideas."

Saber sighed and scratched his chin. "Maybe that's for the best. He's the ringleader. Things might settle down now that Charles is gone. Did Dawn go with Charles?" Dawn was Charles's mate. Saber wondered what Marsh would think of this latest debacle.

"No, rumor says she ripped into him this morning for staying out most of the night and kicked him out of the house," Ben said.

"Rumor?" Saber asked.

"My wife."

Saber struggled to withhold his yawn. "Are we sure he's gone?"

"Well, I saw him drive off after he and Dawn had words a few minutes ago," Ben said. "I wasn't close enough to hear the argument but Judy said she heard everything. Dawn wants to see her grandchildren, but Marsh refuses to let them visit her and Charles."

"I'm going home," Saber said, every muscle in his body screaming with exhaustion. "Emily is waiting for me."

Almost on cue, a siren blasted through the chatter of the remaining shapeshifters and their mates. Charlie McKenzie tore from the parking lot, his fellow cop Laura Adams in the passenger seat. Their mates stared after them in resignation and piled into the same SUV to head home while Agnes and Valerie quick-footed it in their direction.

"Charles Rutherford has set fire to the police station," Agnes informed them.

Saber yawned and turned away.

"Aren't you going to help the cops?" Valerie asked. "Saber?"

Saber stilled, his hands white-knuckling at his sides. He turned to face his fellow councilmembers and straightened his shoulders. "No."

"B-but..." Agnes spluttered.

"If you feel the presence of a councilmember is necessary, one of you can go. I am going home to bed." Saber ignored the flurry of whispers and comments and walked away. Tonight, he'd had enough. He'd deal with any fallout tomorrow.

Chapter Three

Two days later, Saber prowled across the tussock in feline form, gradually picking up speed until he was racing at full strength. His mind seethed with turmoil. Anger. Helplessness. Pain. He felt it all.

Sly had refused visits. Full stop. Charles had left but the feline community remained uneasy while the police station required repairs. Joe wasn't doing well and Emily...

The emotions roiled inside him, combining into doubt and panic. Something had to change between him and Emily before it was too late and their marriage failed. His muscles strained. His lungs labored as he fought the stiff breeze roaring over the brow of the hill. Running didn't help. No matter how fast his sprint, he couldn't outrun his fears.

He was losing Emily.

Anguish swelled inside him and he slowed, realizing he'd instinctively headed for the spot where he and Emily had made love during the heady days of their courtship. He'd known what he'd wanted then. Confidence had filled him as he'd pursued his goals. He'd wanted Emily and done his best to seduce and woo her to his way of thinking. Officially bestowing his mark on Emily and mating with her was the best thing he'd ever done.

He loved her.

It might seem laughable to some, but Emily really completed him. Her presence made him a better man. She pulled him and his brothers together, making them into a big, happy family, one full of love and laughter.

Hell, he didn't know what to do, how to make things better or how to fix the yawning hole between them. Because there was one thing he knew for sure—he couldn't survive without Emily. They were mates, meant to live out their lives together.

Saber came to a halt in the shelter of a large pile of schist, his sides heaving from the exertion. The scent of dried grasses and the underlying, more pungent aroma of the soil, damp from recent rain and cattle filled his lungs. He'd come out here to think, but his mind couldn't get past the fact he was losing Emily and the reality—he'd never felt so powerless in his entire life.

It didn't help that he hadn't been there for her and their unborn daughter when they needed him. That's what killed him most of all. He'd promised to look after Emily and hadn't. He'd failed her.

The ache of inadequacy gnawed at him. Despondently, he padded back into the wind, heading for his vehicle. This time self-sufficiency wasn't going to work. He needed help.

Half an hour later, he walked into Gavin Finley's surgery, halting just inside the door. Kiran, Gavin's assistant, was with him as they worked on a golden retriever.

"Gavin, I need to make an appointment," Saber said. "Can you fit me in?"

"Is there a problem?" Gavin watched Kiran stitch the wound closed.

"No. Yes." His hands curled to fists at his sides while he struggled to ask for assistance. He was the one who fixed problems. He didn't need support. His shoulders slumped forward a fraction.

That was a lie.

He and Emily desperately required help. Saber glanced at Kiran. He'd tried to feel anger at the young tiger shifter because it was his presence that had placed Emily in the path of danger. Logically, he knew Kiran was just as innocent as Emily and their unborn baby. The men who had stormed their house, searching for Kiran, were to blame, and his initial anger had dulled.

"I need to speak with you in private—when you have a moment."

"Kiran and I have another appointment." Gavin glanced at the wall clock. "We should be done by three. Do you want to meet at Storm in a Teacup for a coffee?"

"No," he barked. That was the last thing he wanted. Emily was actually working there today, which was a change from the lethargy and melancholy of the past months. He didn't want Emily to know he was seeing Gavin. "I...could we meet here?"

"Better make it half past three so I have a chance to get something to eat. My stomach is gnawing my backbone."

"I'll bring food and coffee," Saber said. Emily would give him food. They might not talk, they might not socialize with family and friends in the same way they used to, but they did eat, or pretend to, in the case of his mate.

"I NEED TO TALK to you about Emily." Despite the feeling of disloyalty, Saber would do anything to make things right. They'd never be the same as they were before. Saber knew and accepted that. But he refused to believe the empty bubble they'd inhabited for months was all they had in the future. He forced himself to talk, to stumble through and lay out his—their—personal problems in the hope Gavin could help. "She's not getting better. We don't talk anymore. We sleep in the same bed, but that's all. Emily doesn't—won't touch me." A lump built in Saber's throat, the sting of tears coming on him suddenly. "She locks herself in the bathroom and cries. She thinks I don't know. It's like she's retreated to her own world where nothing else exists. I...I don't know how to fix things." Saber squeezed his eyes shut, concentrating fiercely on maintaining his equilibrium when all he wanted to do was howl with the pain.

"You have to give it time." Gavin reached for his hand, making Saber flinch. Instinctively, he tried to pull away, but Gavin held fast, refusing to let him withdraw. "The loss of a baby due to miscarriage is exactly like mourning the loss of a loved one. You both bonded with your baby and pictured what she'd look like. You considered names and set up a nursery. God, Saber. Something like this doesn't go away overnight. Emily needs to grieve and go through all the stages, the initial grief, the anger, the depression and acceptance before she can come out the other side. You both do."

"But how much time?" Saber inhaled and blew out the breath slowly to release the tension residing in every muscle of his body. He'd known this would be difficult. Just talking about their baby girl felt like someone had taken a knife to his gut. "I...we can't keep on like this without our marriage breaking. I can't lose Emily. I can't," Saber finished fiercely. They'd lost enough already.

Gavin frowned, reaching for a pen. Saber watched him tap it on the desk and hoped he'd stop soon, his eyes narrowing as his mind started screaming at him. Everything annoyed him these days and his uncertain temper proved it. His brothers treaded warily, treating him like a wild animal.

"Have you thought about a change of scenery? Sometimes that helps." Gavin paused, as if he were weighing his words.

His prolonged silence sent Saber's alarm bells ringing. He straightened, his spine hitting the back of his wooden chair as he stared at Gavin impassively.

"How are *you* doing?"

"Fine," Saber said in a gruff voice.

Gavin maintained his measured gaze, and Saber struggled to hold everything together. Everyone expected him to remain strong.

"I'm fine," he repeated.

Gavin didn't look as if he believed him. Saber steeled himself for another barrage of questions but they didn't come.

"Why don't you go on holiday? Go to the beach or the mountains—any place where you can be alone together and away from Middlemarch drama. Give yourselves time to mourn and reconnect with each other."

"Emily won't go."

"Maybe you should take matters into your own hands. Organize a holiday and make it so she can't refuse."

Saber nodded slowly, knowing his brothers would pick up the slack for him. All he needed to do was ask them. Emily wouldn't have a problem either. It wasn't as if she was spending much time at Storm in a Teacup these days anyway. "Maybe you're right. Maybe we should take a holiday."

"Great. How does Fiji sound? Lucas Huntingdon mentioned a resort on one of the Fijian Islands the other night when we had dinner together. It's private and exclusive. He's thinking of investing in the resort. I'm sure he can swing a special deal for you."

Fiji. That would mean a plane flight, and he hated flying.

"I can give you something to get through the flight," Gavin said, obviously reading his mind.

Saber nodded again, seduced by the idea of peace and Emily. No council business. No family drama. "I'll ring Lucas tonight."

SMALL TURQUOISE WAVES LAPPED the white sand while a gentle breeze stirred the palm trees, making the fronds rattle musically. A bright orange crab scuttled in front of Emily, the suddenness of his darting run startling her. She let out a girlie squeak of surprise, blushing when Saber laughed.

"It's just a crab," Saber said, steadying her with a brief touch on the shoulder. He swiped a lock of black hair from his face with his free hand, and his faint smile almost reached his eyes. "It won't hurt you."

His touch lasted for fleeting seconds before he moved away and resumed his ambling walk. Emily knew the crab wouldn't hurt her, but she was on edge, the knowledge that Saber wanted to talk truly terrifying her. Things had been difficult between them—strained—since...since... God, she couldn't bear to think about her baby girl. She blinked rapidly, trying to hold back the tears.

People didn't go on holiday to discuss getting a divorce, did they? Besides, he was almost smiling. She didn't think men who wanted a divorce looked as if they wanted to smile. Too bad he was stuck with her because of the feline mark he'd bestowed on her.

Only death would stop their yearning for each other, but that didn't mean they needed to live in the same house. These days she couldn't even look at Saber without recalling the way she'd let him down.

She'd lost their baby, their beautiful daughter.

She'd failed dismally.

Fighting the ache of tears, Emily continued to walk along the sheltered bay at Saber's side. She had no idea how she'd ended up on an almost-deserted Fijian island. No, that wasn't quite true. Saber had maneuvered her, making it impossible for her to refuse. Only twenty-four hours after his announcement, she'd found herself about to board a plane with her friends and family excitedly taking care of the details such as packing and organizing a roster to keep her cafe running smoothly.

She stole a glance at Saber, anxiety tying her stomach in knots. Her hand trembled when she brushed her hair aside and tucked a lock behind her ear. "Why are we here? Why are we in Fiji? You never said what you wanted to talk about." She'd wanted to ask him straight-out if he intended to show his disappointment in her and move out of their home. Like her first husband... Michael hadn't approved of her either, leaving her for his secretary.

"We're having a long-overdue holiday." Saber stopped walking, reached for her hand and tugged until they faced each other. "I thought it would do us both good if we took a break and relaxed."

"And there's no other reason?" Fear made her insistent. She was a defective wife. Michael had told her so. Saber wasn't cruel like her ex. Saber was subtler and that's what scared her most of all. She scanned his face, desperately trying to read him.

Saber hesitated. "No other reason."

Sweat trickled down her back and it wasn't just a product of the heat. Saber had considered his reply carefully. Her mind leapt ahead, trying to work out what he could mean. God, she should ask more questions, but she was frightened of learning the answers. Instead, she wiped the back of her hand across her brow. "It's hot."

"Would you like to go for a swim?"

"I don't have my swimsuit. I'll have to go back to our *bure* to get it." The cute wood and straw huts might appear rustic on the outside, but inside they were pure luxury. The thought heightened the tension churning inside her stomach. She didn't understand why they were in Fiji.

Saber tugged his tank top over his head, and Emily couldn't help but stare. He'd hardly changed in the three years they'd been mates. The breeze had ruffled his shaggy black hair in an attractive manner while his green eyes glowed with an inner fire she hadn't seen for some time. Determination. He had a goal and intended to achieve whatever target he had in mind. She skittered away from the possibilities even though they lurked in her mind like sharks circling a coral reef.

Heck, what would she do if Saber asked for a separation?

"This is our private beach. We don't need swimsuits." Saber removed the last of his clothes and shot her a challenging look. "Come for a swim. It's not safe for me to swim alone."

Emily felt her mouth gape open and she hurriedly closed it again. Her gaze darted the length of his body, and when he laughed softly, she realized her attention had lingered on his groin. Heat filled her cheeks and no doubt stained her face with color.

"Chicken?"

His taunt made her gasp. The teasing light in his eyes reminded her of how it had been in the beginning and the instant attraction between them when they'd first met. Heck, what did she do?

"I can't believe you've turned shy."

"No." The denial shot from her mouth before she could censor it.

"No? So why aren't you taking off your clothes?" His eyes sparkled with challenge and devilment. Unbidden, her fingers went to the buttons of her cotton shirt. The top button slipped free then the second. She glanced at him and watched his dark brows rise, upping the dare. Emily averted her gaze, huffing out a breath at the same time. She rapidly undid the rest of her buttons and slid the shirt off her shoulders. They'd been together for three years, knew each other intimately, yet this felt like the first time all over again. Once again, her mind leapt to the reasons Saber had arranged this uncharacteristic holiday. He wasn't acting as if he wanted to walk away. Emily swallowed the lump of nerves tightening her throat. Maybe she could seduce him? Maybe that would help? Reaching behind her, she unfastened her bra and tossed it on the sand. Without looking at Saber, she kicked off her sandals and scrambled from the rest of her clothes, trying not to wince at the stretch marks and pale skin he'd see.

"Emily." The alpha note in his voice called to her, made her look without volition. He smiled with approval and stretched out a hand for her to take.

Confusion was an understatement. She hesitated then took his hand. A frisson of heat sped from her fingertips and up her arm. The sun beat down, warming her all over. Skin that had never seen the sun glowed a dazzling white. An excited little blip jolted her, much like the first time they'd touched.

Ah memories. Her heart twisted with anguish as she stepped into the sea. No matter how much she wanted Saber, things could never be the same, not after all that had happened. She had to remember that. She couldn't pass the blame to Kiran or anyone else. The sole responsibility for her lost baby rested with her.

"You're beautiful, Emily."

Her breath hitched and she glanced at him in surprise. What the heck was he doing? Thinking? Slightly bemused, she allowed him to tug her deeper into the sun-warmed tropical water. It lapped at her thighs then her waist, caressing her skin like smooth, glossy satin. When they reached breast-depth, Saber halted and turned to her, grasping her upper arms to hold her in place. Not that she could have moved. The light in his green eyes stole her breath, weakened her knees.

He intended to kiss her. The knowledge seared her, making her mouth open in shock. Saber hadn't kissed her, hadn't touched her for weeks. She tried to remember the last time and came up empty. Make that months. Emily bit her bottom lip. The non-touching wasn't exactly his fault. At first, she'd been too distraught. Numb from the loss of their baby. And now it was too late to bridge the gap. She didn't know how.

Unaccountably nervous, she tugged at the ends of her long hair. It hung like brown rat's tails, partially concealing her breasts. It needed a cut. Something else she'd ignored recently.

"If you don't want me to kiss you, tell me now."

Her gasp was audible above the lap of the waves. His fingers tightened on her upper arms to a point shy of pain. She stared up at him, peeking from between lowered lashes. He looked...hungry. Predatory like the dangerous cat he was. Without waiting for her to reply, he lowered his head, closing the distance between them. Their lips met, tentative and cautious, much like a first kiss. That comparison faded rapidly as Saber deepened the contact, drawing her closer so his muscular chest crushed her breasts. An intense burst of heat hit her, swirling through her body. Her heart lurched painfully, and a moan escaped as he devoured her, wrapping his arms around her as if she were a treasured possession.

In shock, Emily clutched his shoulders, allowing him to push his tongue into her mouth, taking the kiss from hesitant to carnal. After wavering, she went with the moment, embracing it with everything she had, grateful for the contact when she'd thought Saber detested her and wanted her gone.

His low groan and the dig of his cock told her she'd engaged his interest. Then she realized her fingertips stroked his marking site. Horrified, she jerked her hand away from the fleshy pad of skin between shoulder and neck.

"Hell, I want you so much. Please let me make love to you." His husky words should have appeased her fears. No such luck. They terrified her, filled her with doubt. She buried her head against his shoulder, and he must have taken that as consent. He lowered his head to nibble the delicate skin of her neck. His tongue drifted over her mark and the fight drained out of her, replaced by a searing desire she hadn't felt for months.

He continued to lave her mark, using the sensitive spot to play her like an instrument. Emily closed her eyes and clung to him, glorying in his touches. She hadn't realized how starved she'd been for touch, how lonely.

"I can't wait. I'm so sorry. I can't take it slow. I need you so bad." Saber lifted her easily, parting her legs. He guided his shaft to her entrance and pushed inside before letting her weight do the rest.

Emily winced at the slight pain. She wanted him and had thought her body would do the rest, preparing for his possession. Not so.

"Hell, I'm sorry," Saber whispered after registering her flinch.

"No, don't stop." She gripped his biceps with urgency, instinctively knowing if they stopped now things would become even more uncomfortable between them. They stared at each other, the turquoise water rocking their bodies. It felt warm and silky, the idea of making love outdoors where anyone could see very decadent. A turn-on.

Saber kissed her fiercely, their teeth clashing before he angled his mouth a fraction more for the perfect fit. A purr vibrated deep in his throat, the sexy sound relaxing Emily. Saber slid deeper into her, and they both sighed.

"Wrap your legs around my hips and hold on to my shoulders." He placed her hands on his shoulders when she was slow to respond to his order. "That's it. Now use the buoyancy of the water. Yeah," he purred. "Perfect."

The feel of his cock stretching muscles and tissues unused for some time sent a curl of arousal spiraling through her pussy. She rose up and sank back down, her eyes fluttering closed to concentrate on the building pleasure. It felt so good being with Saber like this. So good. Part of her had missed him, but she hadn't realized the full extent of the crack in their relationship until he'd touched her intimately again. Emily admitted it—she couldn't let him go. Despite the aching silence between them, she could never stand aside and let him move on to another woman.

Never.

Emily quickened her pace, rising and falling until hot, sensual flames licked every inch of her flesh.

"Emily. God, you feel so good wrapped around my cock. So tight and wet. I can't...oh hell." His entire body shook as he climaxed hard.

She felt the splash of wetness deep inside her and the faint pulse of his cock as he burrowed his head in the crook of her neck. His mouth fastened over her mark, his tongue moving over it in a soft, tormenting stroke. It felt good. Heck, it felt great, but it wasn't enough. Saber softened and lifted her away from him.

"Come with me," he said.

Emily opened her mouth to complain and snapped it shut again. Complaining wasn't the way to get back in Saber's good books. She should count her blessings. At least he was touching her again. He dragged her to shallow water and turned to grin when they reached the shore.

"Perfect."

Before she could ask what was so perfect about feeling sexually frustrated, he swept her off her feet and placed her on the sand. Seconds later he joined her. Bewildered by the swift move, she blinked. A wave ran to shore, the white foam rushing over their bodies. Saber chuckled and let the water sweep them higher up the beach. He leaned over, caging her beneath his body and started kissing her. He devoured her mouth, sweeping aside the protest forming on her lips. They were on a beach where anyone could see them. She pushed at his shoulders until he lifted his head.

"Shouldn't we get dressed?" She cast a swift glance left and right, reassuring herself they were alone.

"I told you. It's a secluded beach. Our beach for the entire month."

"But I'll get sunburned."

"Not if you stop protesting and let me have my way."

He wanted to have his way with her. *Be still my heart.* "Haven't you already had your way with me?" she snapped.

"Ask me at the end of the month." His grin faded, replaced by the open determination she recalled from the days of their courtship. He'd wanted her and had courted her until she came around to his way of thinking. He'd been sweet yet relentless. "By the end of our holiday you should have your answer."

"What answer?"

"That's for you to find out." He snared her gaze, and where she expected anger, she received a grin. "Shut up and kiss me." His mouth descended and he sealed their lips, their talking seemingly done for the moment.

Confusion pounded along with her heartbeat as the kiss changed from persuading to sweet. Her blood seemed to thicken in her veins. Sweet mercy. They hadn't kissed like this in forever. Saber's brothers or their wives always interrupted or they had visitors. At the time, Emily hadn't minded because she'd become part of a family—the family she'd always wanted. Then she'd fallen pregnant and she'd never been happier.

She should've known something would go wrong.

Saber lifted his head. "Stop thinking so hard."

"I'm not."

"You are. You've checked out on me again. It's insulting and makes me think you don't want me. Do you know what that sort of thing does to a man?"

Emily gaped at him in shock. Not want him? Did he have rocks in his head? It was him who'd engineered this holiday. It was Saber who said they needed to talk. "I...no, that's not true." Of course she wanted him!

"Good to know," he said gruffly, and started to nuzzle her neck. He kissed the delicate spot behind her ear and nipped her throat. One big hand caressed her breast. Since her pregnancy they'd become more sensitive and she gasped at the bungee of sensation that shot to her clit. She stirred, wriggling a little, caressing Saber's back, her hand sliding down his spine to come to a rest on his rump. "No touching," he ordered in a husky voice. "Hands above your head."

Emily frowned, becoming more and more bewildered by his behavior.

"Hands above your head," he repeated, his fingers a frustrating inch away from her nipple. She wanted to experience the hit of pleasure again.

"You're the one who's gonna get a sunburned arse." She aimed for smug but didn't pull it off. Instead she sounded bewildered, which was exactly the way she felt.

"Are you refusing to follow my instructions?"

"Yes." An imp inside Emily decided to act out. She had no idea what she was doing, so off-balance she didn't know what to think or how to react to this resolute Saber.

His eyes darkened. "Are you sure you want to do that?"

"Y-yes." No, she wasn't sure at all. She had no idea what she was doing.

Saber grinned then, moving so quickly she scarcely had time to blink. A squeak erupted from her as he positioned her over his knee. He caressed her buttocks with his callused hand—a farmer's hand, rough from the day-to-day workload.

She'd hardly registered the caress when he lifted his hand. She felt the warmth of the sun, the faint kiss of the breeze—then he smacked her.

"Ow!" She reared up in shock, the masculine grin she witnessed flabbergasting her even more. She attempted to wriggle free, but he held her firmly. His fingers brushed across the stinging flesh of her buttock.

"That's for disobeying me."

Disobeying? What the hell? Before she could say a word, he smacked her again—two rapid taps in separate places. Heat spread over her butt, the sting of pain clearing quickly to bring a new, surprising sensation. Holy Hannah. She'd heard of spanking and immediately decided it was way outside her comfort level and a kink she never wanted to experience. Maybe she should rethink this, along with a few other things?

There was a long silence, broken only by a gull flying overhead and the swish of the incoming waves. A quiver went through her as she cataloged the feelings pulsing through her body.

"I've never disobeyed you."

"No?" Three, swift smacks rained down on her stinging buttocks.

This time there was no mistake. She groaned and it wasn't with pain. When the third smack came, she lifted into it, embarrassingly aware of the surge of juices trickling from between her legs.

"Do you like that, Emily?"

"No," she blurted, aghast at admitting the truth.

"And this is for lying to me." Another series of smacks sent heat skittering across her backside, the vibrations going all the way to her clit. Before she could analyze the combined pain and pleasure, she felt Saber's hand cupping her burning buttocks. He trailed his fingers gently across her singing flesh. Emily couldn't prevent a quiver of pleasure. "You like this. I can smell your pleasure."

"Maybe." Heat suffused her face, and she was glad he couldn't see her expression. Heck, she'd never get used to his sneaky feline senses. It was difficult to keep changes in her body to herself. He'd even known she was pregnant before she'd realized it herself. She pressed her lips together to contain her sudden flash of humor. He was certainly enjoying himself because his cock was digging into her.

"Let's see, shall we?" Saber ran a finger between her legs, a distinct liquid sound making her blush harder. "Good, I was right."

Before she knew it, he'd arranged her on all fours. He moved behind and entered her with one hard thrust. This time there was no pain. Only pleasure. He retreated and invaded, filling her with leisurely strokes while he toyed with her swollen bud. Teasing and stroking her until she whimpered and trembled against him.

"Saber," she whispered, pushing back into his thrusts.

He rocked into her again and the tension inside her snapped. Her pussy pulsed around his cock, pleasure fizzing through her veins with each unhurried pass of his fingers. She moaned out loud, shattering under the maelstrom of sensations.

"That's it, kitten. You feel good. I like the way your cunt squeezes my cock."

His dirty talk set another smaller series of pulses in motion. Saber cursed softly and slammed into her, gripping her hips as he repeated the move then stilled, fully impaled. His husky groan of completion filled Emily with satisfaction. Not even the painful grip of his hands at her hips dulled her delight in the moment. It seemed they hadn't lost the knack when it came to good sex. She just hoped they could solve the rest of their problems as easily.

CHAPTER FOUR

Saber pulled out of Emily, feeling better than he had in days. Hell, he was almost grateful to Leo and Isabella for the advice they'd given him at the airport, along with the interesting bag of sex toys. *If all else fails, spank her. Make her see sense,* Leo had whispered to him when they said goodbye.

He stood and held out his hand, helping her to rise. "Come on. Let's go and have a shower."

"I seem to have sand in some interesting places."

A ripple of pure pleasure went through Saber as Emily actually took his hand. When they reached their pile of clothes, he scooped them up.

"Aren't we going to get dressed?"

Not if he had his way. Saber intended to keep her naked for as much of the month as he could. "We're going to have a shower. There's no point dressing."

"At least let me put on my sandals. The sand's hot."

They paused for Emily to thrust her feet into the sandals and continued to their luxurious *bure*.

Buoyed by their lovin' outdoors, he led Emily into the bathroom. The shower was huge and plenty big enough for sensual play. He had something else in mind though for their afternoon—something more comfortable. After tossing the clothes aside, he knelt to remove Emily's footwear and urged her to turn on the shower. Soon the water poured from the dual showerheads, making quick work of the sand when they stepped under the spray.

Saber lathered lavender gel on a washcloth. "Turn around. Let me do your back."

She hesitated where once she would have followed his direction without delay. It hurt—her lack of...trust. Yeah, trust. Once she'd believed in him completely. He hoped the intimacy and confidence that came with sex might be the thing to fix the breach between them.

"I've never done anything to warrant your hesitation. Do you trust me?"

Her eyes rounded. "Of course I trust you."

"Show some faith. Let me wash you." He watched her audible swallow and felt his temper strain at the leash. If he could get his hands on the bastard who had injured Emily and their baby, he'd kill him all over again with his bare hands. Reining in his emotions, he waited for her to obey.

Slowly she turned to present her back.

"Part your legs for me." Saber breathed out in relief when the hesitation was scarcely noticeable this time. He washed her back and moved down to her backside, taking care to use gentle strokes because he knew her buttocks would feel tender. He'd enjoyed spanking her, but the fucking—lovemaking had been even better. He slipped a sudsy hand between her legs, using a teasing stroke. He didn't want to get her off again yet, but keeping her on edge was all part of the plan. "Shall I tell you what I'm going to do with you for the rest of the afternoon?"

"What?" The cautious reply made him smile. He pressed a kiss to the middle of her spine and curved his hands around her body to cup her breasts. A perfect handful.

"I'm going to start right from the beginning. We'll lie on the bed together and make out."

Emily turned to face him, a question in her expression. "Kissing?"

"I like to kiss you." And he hadn't done it enough recently. "I'm gonna cup your face in my hands and kiss you. Soft kisses on your eyelids. A peck on your nose. I might nibble your chin or lick around your luscious mouth."

"That is a lot of kissing."

At least she sounded intrigued.

"I'm going to slide my tongue across the seam of your mouth, take a taste. Maybe nip your bottom lip. Then we'll kiss. Slow kisses. Light kisses. Kisses with tongue. We'll kiss for a long time." Saber brushed his fingers over her pink lips. "And that's just for starters." He washed her breasts, cupping them with soapy hands. God, she was beautiful. He'd thought so the first time he saw her and his feelings hadn't changed. This holiday had to work. He sluiced the last of the soap away and briskly washed himself. "That's it. Let's go."

Saber turned off the water and nudged Emily out of the glass stall. He grabbed a towel and blotted the droplets of water from her body.

"Wait for me on the bed."

Emily frowned. "You're awfully bossy lately."

Because he was frightened she'd leave him if he didn't force the issue. He'd tried to support her, be strong, but he hurt too. He mourned their child as much as Emily did. "Is submitting to my instructions such a bad thing?" Hell, the last thing he wanted to do was hurt or scare her.

"Nooo."

Saber frowned inwardly. He needed to keep her too busy to think. "So, if I retrieved the four silk scarves from the bag of sex toys Leo and Isabella gave me and tied you to the bed you wouldn't have a problem with that?"

"Leo and Isabella gave you sex toys?"

"At the airport." He grinned as he recalled Leo's wink-wink, nudge-nudge routine while telling him about the sex toys. At the time he'd felt like throttling his brother, but he'd come around to his way of thinking. The bag held all sorts of erotic possibilities.

"I saw the three of you in a huddle."

Saber grinned. "On the bed, Emily. We're going to play with some of the toys now."

Her bottom lip jutted out. "What about the kisses?"

"Don't worry. There will be plenty of those to go around. On the bed. Now."

Emily's heart started to race. This holiday was shaping up into something quite different from what she'd anticipated. She didn't understand exactly what Saber was up to, but he obviously still desired her. Maybe she'd go along with whatever he wanted. He wasn't acting like a man intent on separation. Michael had stated his intentions upfront, so perhaps her fears about their relationship were ungrounded.

With another quick glance at Saber's impassive face, Emily strolled into the bedroom, putting a sway in her step as she headed for the bed. In the past she'd done seduction well. She could do it again if she put her mind to it.

She dropped onto the firm mattress and rolled to the middle of the huge bed to wait for Saber. He took his sweet time. When he prowled to the bedroom, her nerves hummed with trepidation. What exactly did he intend to do with her? The bag of toys could contain anything. *Everything*.

He stopped by the wardrobe, the door creaking when he opened it. A zipper sounded, and the pace of her heartbeat cranked up a little further.

"Close your eyes."

Emily followed the instruction, trying to breathe evenly and keep her nerves under control. Every sense intensified with the lack of vision.

"Ah," Saber said.

"Ah what?" The unknown was turning into a many-headed monster. She knew Leo's sense of humor and the knowledge did little to reassure her.

"Nothing sinister. Keep your eyes closed."

He started kissing her, just as he'd described earlier. He cupped her face with his work-rough hands and brushed kisses over her closed eyes. He licked around her mouth and fused their lips in a toe-curling kiss. Tender yet intimate, it stole her breath, made her pulse race, and above all, his caress gave her hope. He laced their fingers together while he continued to stoke a fire in her. Gradually he upped the pace until he was devouring her mouth. The entire time he held her hands, grounding and making her feel connected. He gentled the contact, slowly easing back until their mouths barely brushed. Lost in a sensual haze, Emily floated with the pleasure.

Saber separated their hands. "Keep your eyes closed," he reminded her as he moved.

With Saber no longer touching her, every nerve ending pulsed in awareness. She heard what sounded like a bottle opening. The harsh wheeze confirmed it. The mattress depressed and she felt him straddle her hips. Her skin prickled as she imagined him studying her body, her breasts.

At least he couldn't call her fat like Michael had because she'd dropped a lot of weight in the last few months. Most of her clothes hung on her like unattractive sacks. Not that she cared, although she had to admit, looking like a bag lady probably wasn't the way to keep a mate onside. Perhaps that was why Saber had insisted on skinny-dipping. Maybe her one-piece swimsuit offended him.

"Stop frowning." Something in his tone suggested she'd upset him again. Checking out, he'd called it. She really didn't mean to, but her mind sprinted all over the place and every thought reminded her of her failure.

"I'm not." Emily wiped her expression clean and denied everything.

"You know what happens when you lie."

Spanking. A bolt of arousal shot through her at the thought of Saber striking her backside again. Heck, if it felt that good all the time, she'd be happy for him to spank her. The beginnings of a grin tugged at her mouth.

Saber didn't give her a chance to deny her lie. Liquid drizzled across her breasts, warm and fragrant. A hint of sandalwood and spicy cinnamon teased her nostrils. Her skin tickled as the liquid ran down the curve of her breast. His large hands dispersed the oil, rotating in firm, circular strokes across her breasts and straying to her shoulders. He moved teasingly close to her nipples, the sensual tension that had dissipated, growing again. His touch felt so decadent. He'd always touched her, made her feel good in the past, but he'd never taken such care or ordered her around as he had today. It was kind of hot, but once again, Emily wondered what it meant. She'd taken to dissecting every action, every word because the future frightened her so much.

She sighed when his fingers drifted closer to her areola and she felt her nipple pull to a taut nub. "Saber," she whispered, his name a silent demand for more.

"If you want more, Emily, you need to tell me. I don't want a passive lover."

A sliver of fear struck her at his words. She'd certainly been passive lately. "I don't understand. You liked my submission earlier."

"There's a difference between passive and submissive."

There was? "Explain." The one word held all the tension she felt inside.

"Passive tells me you don't care either way. I could be anyone, any man. You're just going through the motions. Submissive is different because you choose to give yourself to my care. It means you want and desire me."

"I want you," Emily said sharply, panic stripping away her previous calm.

"Do you?"

Emily opened her eyes, more disturbed by the strange note in Saber's voice than she cared to admit. "I want you to tug on my nipples. Pinch them and give me a hint of pain." Her heart thudded against her ribs as they stared at each other.

"Close your eyes again."

"Why?"

"I want you to concentrate on the tactile sensations, the pleasure. I want you to relax. You haven't done much of that lately."

Emily held his determined gaze, let out a huff of exasperation and finally did as he ordered. Immediately he started to massage her breasts, his even strokes soothing the tension bubbling through her mind. This interaction with Saber might be terrifying, but it had forced her to focus and concentrate. The emptiness didn't feel quite as bad and despondency didn't cut so deep.

His fingers crept closer to her nipples, a bolt of sensation streaking through her when he gave a light tug. Her breath caught when he followed up with a pinch. A shard of pain echoed in her pussy and a soft groan escaped. His palms moved in firm circles above both nipples then he tweaked them hard. The burning twinge of pain heated her entire body and she bit her lip to keep from calling out, from begging for more.

This caution was also something new. He'd told her to ask for what she wanted, to quit her passive behavior, but did he really want that? He'd always directed their lovemaking, telling or showing her what he wanted her to do.

He shifted his weight downward, his hand leaving her breast. More oil trickled on her heated skin, running into her navel. She shivered with anticipation, determined to keep her fears at the back of her mind.

"Part your legs for me."

She followed his instruction, jumping a little when he drizzled more oil over the folds of her sex. Emily gave a fleeting thought to the sheets before his attentions distracted her along with a tingling sensation where the oil hit her aroused flesh. Saber's fingers followed the flow of the oil, whispered across her swollen folds. She trembled, imagining the expression on his face as he studied her responses to his touch. His eyes would darken. They might bear a glint of humor or his face might pull tight with need.

Instead of teasing her, he seemed bent on arousing her. A thick finger pushed into her sheath while another circled her clit. A buzzing sound started without warning, and she felt him insert something into her pussy.

"Does that feel good? Tell me."

"Yes, it feels good." A vibrator?

"Emily." Her name held a wealth of disappointment, making her wonder exactly what he wanted from her.

After all these years together, she should've known.

"Give me specifics. Does it feel better if I do this? Or this?" He removed the vibrator and trailed it over her clit.

A double jolt of pleasure took her by surprise when he pressed his fingers against the front wall of her vagina and circled her clit with the vibrator. "Oh yes. Do that again. Yes, right there."

"Words, Emily. Give me words. Talk dirty to me."

A flush of heat filled her cheeks and seeped down her throat to her chest. He wanted frank language? She could do that. "I want you to fuck me with your finger and touch the sweet spot—yes! Right there." The heat intensified inside her, a flash detonating in her sex.

"Better," he acknowledged, laughter shading his voice. "Give me more. Nothing you ask for will shock me."

Confusion settled in Emily and refused to let her fully relax. What the heck was he trying to prove? Had he become bored with their sex life? No, scratch that. Of course he had because they hadn't exactly had a sex life since...since...

Her breath whooshed out while she battled a sudden realization. She had gone through something similar with Michael. They'd gone on a holiday together, one that she'd arranged in the hope they'd rekindle the heady times of their honeymoon. A shudder went through her and it had nothing to do with Saber. It was stone-cold fear. What if Saber had met someone else?

No. She shoved the thought away as soon as it crystallized in her mind. Saber wasn't like that. He wasn't sneaky and wouldn't treat her or any other woman in that manner. No, Saber was honest. She trusted him completely, which meant there was something else afoot here. The last thing she wanted to do was lose him. Then she really would be alone.

"Emily." The hard tone in his voice sent chills rioting through her. She froze and opened her eyes, consternation pounding in concert with her elevated pulse rate. He removed his fingers from her pussy, and her heart thumped hard. Worry joined her panic when he switched off the vibrator. His face—she had to see his expression to try to make sense of things.

"What?" She had never sounded so timid in all her life, and the sardonic curl of his lips told her he'd picked up her diffidence.

"There are three people in bed with us. Kick the third out or I'll walk."

CHAPTER FIVE

EMILY STARED AT SABER in acute shock. She scrambled to an upright position, her heart pounding so loudly she could scarcely hear herself think. "You think I'm having an affair? Are you crazy?" Her voice rose toward the end of her sentence and her eyes prickled with a tightness that signaled imminent tears. "How could you think that I would..." she trailed off, words deserting her in the face of his accusation.

"I never said you were having an affair." He scrubbed a hand over his face and the anger drained out of him. "I said there were three people in bed with us. You keep checking out. I hate making love to you when you're not in the moment with me."

Emily swallowed, the shocks coming one after the other. Saber wasn't one for a lot of deep discussions. Oh, she knew and sensed his feelings, and lately she'd been aware of his turmoil. Part of it came through the mate bond. The other part she surmised from observations and the fact she'd lived with him for several years. "I don't understand."

Saber climbed to his feet and started pacing. His laugh held bitterness. "Of course you don't. If you think I'm not hurting, that I don't wish I'd been there that day." He whirled to face her, his expression almost savage with the cat shimmering across his face. "I'm going for a run."

"Don't you think you'll need some clothes?" She used a teasing tone, but instead of alleviating some of the tenseness, it served to fuel more. A chill stalked down her spine.

"I'm running in feline form."

"But someone might see."

"Let them," he snarled.

Emily didn't think she could feel yet another shock, but his words caused a ripple of unease. If there was one thing Saber was very careful about, it was letting strangers witness his feline form. When she thought about it, she was still surprised he'd taken the initial plunge during their

71

courtship and showed her his other form. When it came to safety and keeping feline secrets, he verged on paranoid. With just cause. It was easy to imagine the interest feline shifters would engender in the scientific world.

"Okay," she said. "How long will you be gone?" She wanted to know when she should start worrying. She gnawed her bottom lip while she waited for his reply.

His face seemed to soften at her words. "A couple of hours. I need to do some thinking."

"Saber, I have never looked at another man. Never."

"I know," he said, and he crossed the distance separating them, coming to a halt by the bed. Leaning over, he kissed her. It was a gentle kiss yet held a touch of restrained passion that reassured her as words couldn't. "I've arranged a massage session for you. I thought you could use it tomorrow, but why don't you go up to reception and see if they can fit you in this afternoon?" He turned away before she could reply. "And order our dinner while you're up there. Something substantial. You know what I like. We'll eat up in the restaurant tonight."

Before she could reply, he disappeared out the door. Mind in turmoil, she slumped against the fluffy pillows at the head of the bed. If he didn't think she was cheating on him, then what did he mean?

Their lovemaking had been incredible, even better than she remembered. It had been when her mind wandered that he'd transformed from lover to icy stranger. Emily sighed. Saber was right. She had zoned out, taking her head from the present and letting her thoughts drift. Maybe she should come right out and ask him if he resented her because she'd lost their baby.

For a long time she'd even wondered if she could have children. She still remembered the intense relief when she'd fallen pregnant. Saber loved children, and it was so important for the feline community to increase in numbers. Yet he'd never put any pressure on her when it had taken time. He'd showered her with love and support, but things had changed now. She'd lost their baby girl. What if she could never have a child? What would happen to their marriage then?

SABER SHIFTED BENEATH A coconut palm. Assured by management that no one would intrude on their secluded beach, he didn't even search the shadows for voyeurs.

He called up his feline and let the change take him, embracing the pain and discomfort as muscles, sinew and bone reshaped to black leopard.

In a slow lope, he traveled across the white sand, his mind full of thoughts. He'd let his frustration get the better of him earlier. He'd tried to bite his tongue, but Emily had pissed him off with the way she'd obviously been miles away. One minute she was enjoying his ministrations then she'd drifted off to god knew where in her thoughts. He'd started to feel like a third wheel. It was a familiar place, and he resented the hell out of her for making him feel this way—about as useful as tits on a bull.

Hell, he knew she wasn't having an affair. He knew there wasn't another man in her life. It was the baby—their baby—that filled her mind. Fuck, there had to be something wrong with him that he resented a baby. Emily had been so excited when she'd learned of her pregnancy. So had he, elation filling him while he and Emily prepared a nursery and discussed names for their daughter. Saber increased his speed, trying to outrun his pain. Their baby would never know how much they'd loved her.

Saber hit the water, a wave splashing into his face and making his nose tickle. He sneezed and leaped over the next wave, jumping back into the turquoise water.

Emily had to face facts. Their baby had died, but they were both still alive. He needed his wife, the affectionate and warm woman he'd fallen in love with almost at first sight. God, he was jealous. How the hell could he be jealous of a baby, one who had never even taken a breath of air, at that? What kind of a man did that make him?

It made him human. Gavin had told him they both had to mourn. Logically, he understood the concept, but it didn't make it any easier to accept.

Back to Emily. Saber angled his body so he entered the shallower water and picked up his pace. He needed patience. He'd have to start over. If today had proved one thing, it was that they were still sexually compatible. Leo and Isabella obviously knew what they were doing when they'd given him the bag of toys. Mind made up, he continued his run, this time enjoying his surroundings and the warmth of the sun as it beat down on his black fur. He'd go with sexual hijinks and fill Emily with pleasure so deep that she'd focus on nothing else except him.

Outside the *bure*, he shook the sand and seawater from his coat and shifted to human form. Emily wasn't there, but she'd left him a note.

I rang reception and was able to book in a massage. I should be back around four.

Love Emily.

Saber read the note with approval. Part of him had expected to find her still in the *bure*, staring sightlessly at the wall. That she'd taken his suggestion brought a sense of satisfaction. The *Love Emily* bit didn't hurt either. Affection of any kind had been sadly lacking in their lives recently. Something else he intended to change. These days, if he touched her, even in a casual manner, she flinched. Emily needed to get past that. She had to learn she was safe with him. The thought made him pause.

Charlie and Laura, friends and local cops, had told him there was nothing he could have done to change the outcome. The man after Kiran would have killed them all given the opportunity. Gavin had said something along the same lines. Survivors' guilt was a powerful thing. If he wanted to help Emily, he had to push thoughts like that aside. They had to accept the horrid past and move on with their lives.

Saber padded to the bathroom and took a quick shower. Once he'd dried himself, he returned to the bedroom and flung himself on the bed. Emily shouldn't be much longer. He considered the sex toys in his possession and made plans. He worked much better with a goal in sight. He knew exactly what he wanted—a happy life with Emily.

When it came down to it, Saber realized he didn't need children to validate his existence. If they happened that was a bonus, but Emily was more important to him than anything else. He wondered if he should tell her that and shied from the idea. It probably wasn't something she wanted to hear right now.

Sex would bring them together, the physical closeness. The connection—if he could keep her thoughts focused on him. A burst of sensation zapped through his veins. His cock started to fill. Lazily, he caressed it, letting the sensations build while he fantasized about what he could do to Emily, what they could do to each other. Minutes passed and his shaft lengthened, his balls tightening. His eyes closed as he fell into the fantasy, the pleasure.

A soft sound of surprise made his eyes fly open. Emily hovered in the doorway, the faint flush in her cheeks telling of her embarrassment. He considered her a moment longer and casually stroked his cock from base to tip. Her attention was riveted to his length and the stroke of his hand. Okay, maybe not embarrassment. That could be interest.

"Come in," he said, his words low and husky.

Her blush intensified. "I've never seen you do that before."

Saber paused. "I never have time to relax like this when I'm at home. I'm either with my brothers or with you. Why don't you come over here?"

"Only if you keep going," Emily said, surprising him with the note of curiosity in her voice.

Saber grinned. "Would you like me to give you a blow-by-blow description?"

"Yes. I never knew it would be so sexy watching you touch yourself."

The lazy pleasure rippling through Saber ratcheted up a notch at her words. "You can watch me anytime, kitten." Hell, if he'd known how hot he'd get under her attentive gaze he would have tried this earlier. Weeks ago. With his gaze on her, he continued to stroke his cock from root to flared head and back again. He watched as she moved closer to perch on the end of the bed, and scrutinized the flick of her pink tongue as she licked her bottom lip. "Do you want to touch?"

"No, I want to watch. Go on, tell me what you're doing. Give me a running commentary."

The minx was throwing his earlier words back at him. Her teasing brought a rush of hope. All he needed to do was find a way to communicate, a way for them to get past their grief. Saber knew the tragedy of losing their baby would always be there, but it didn't need to rule their lives. Next time— He broke off the thought and stopped stroking his cock.

"What's wrong?"

"Nothing." He aimed for casual and didn't quite make it. They hadn't used condoms earlier. Birth control hadn't even occurred to him. Fuck, he didn't think he could handle Emily getting pregnant again. A ripple of fear made his dick soften.

"Something is wrong," Emily insisted. "I'm not blind. Besides, you've gone all soft and floppy."

"Floppy?" The word burst from him along with a bark of startled laughter. Only Emily had the ability to surprise him and make him laugh this way. "I have enough wood to get the job done."

"I'd ask you to prove it, but I feel so relaxed from the massage I think I'd be the floppy one. That doesn't mean you shouldn't carry on," she added.

Saber thought about avoiding her earlier question and discounted the idea. Avoiding talking is what had landed them in the emotional turmoil. He took a deep breath. "We didn't use any birth control earlier."

"Does it matter?" she asked carefully. Her gaze darted from his, and his stomach sank. God, why hadn't he kept his big mouth shut?

"Do you want to get pregnant again?" Saber's heart twisted when she turned away, stood and moved to the wardrobe.

"Our dinner reservation is at six thirty. If we go soon, we have time for a pre-dinner cocktail. I'd like one of those fruity ones with a little umbrella." The coat hangers rattled as she selected a dress to wear for dinner.

Saber cursed inwardly, no longer interested in getting off. Frustration hammered through him, finding an outlet in clenched fists. Dammit, he wasn't going to let her get away with this. They were going to talk if it was the last thing they did. And they were going to have sex again—lots of sex, either with or without condoms.

It made him realize that, despite his fears for Emily's safety, he would like to try for another baby. He'd loved seeing the changes in her body, the swell of her stomach and the increased tenderness of her breasts. He'd loved feeling their daughter kick. Yeah, another baby might not be such a bad idea—if that was what Emily wanted as well.

Leo and Isabella had added a box of assorted novelty condoms to the goodies, and he'd use them if he needed to, but he wouldn't forgo sex with Emily, not since that seemed to be the only way they could communicate.

Emily walked into the bathroom, still slightly steamy so Saber must have had a shower after his run. Did she want to get pregnant again? Saber's question had taken her by surprise. All this time she'd thought he'd blamed her for losing their baby, for being in the wrong place at the wrong time. But a few things he'd said since they'd arrived here didn't make sense. They certainly didn't add up to separation.

She wiped the foggy mirror with her hand and scowled at her reflection. She hadn't even thought about the lack of birth control. They hadn't used anything for a long time, so it wasn't something that had struck her as odd. She loved the feel of Saber inside her with nothing between them.

After turning on the shower, she stepped into the glass cubicle. Mindful of the time, she washed briskly. She dried off and realized she'd brought her sundress with her, but in her hurry to escape Saber, she'd forgotten to get a pair of panties.

"Bother." Emily smoothed on vanilla and cinnamon body lotion before applying a little makeup.

"Something wrong?" Saber's gaze wandered down her body before returning to her face. The hunger he didn't try to hide made her stomach buck and her breasts prickle with anticipation. Wow, that didn't look like a man who wasn't interested.

"I don't need a bra with this dress but I forgot my panties. Won't be long."

"Don't bother with panties," he said, and he couched his words as an order. "I want you to wear these for me."

Emily stared at the two round balls sitting in the palm of his hand. Wear? Did one wear Ben Wa balls?

"Part your legs so I can put them in for you."

Saber didn't give her a choice. His brows rose while he waited, his will implacable. Slowly she widened her stance. With the ease of familiarity, he ran his fingers down her slit, stroking softly over her clit until warmth sizzled inside her. Emily bit back her groan of pleasure with difficulty. Since they'd made love earlier, she'd thought a lot about sex. Walking in on Saber pleasuring himself had only heightened the arousal sizzling through her sensitized body.

With deft fingers, he inserted the balls into her pussy. "Perfect," he said. "I'm going to enjoy thinking about you wearing them for me tonight."

Emily took an experimental step and heard a faint tinkle. They felt surprisingly comfortable and a bit naughty. "What if they fall out? I've never tried these before, but Tomasine said she had some and they fell out when she and Felix went out for dinner. Felix thought it was funny. Tomasine said it was plain embarrassing."

Saber made a choking sound deep in his throat. "Damn, when was that? Felix didn't say a word."

"Quite right. Men shouldn't go around telling tales."

Saber chuckled and tugged on her hand, indicating she should follow him into the bedroom. He plucked her dress off the hanger and took it with them. The Ben Wa balls tinkled a little but felt secure when she walked.

"Get dressed. Just the dress," he said.

"But what if I fall flat on my face? I don't want everyone to see my bare backside."

"You won't fall," Saber said, "because I'll be at your side to catch you. I won't let you fall."

BY THE END OF their dinner, Emily wasn't worried about the Ben Wa balls falling out. Neither was she worried about falling over. No, the thing that concerned her most was leaving an obvious wet spot on her dress. It was a combination of Saber's full attention and the Ben Wa balls. Her stomach quivered, and she bit down on her lip, trying to contain the arousal surging through her body. Her breasts felt heavy and oh so tender. Her pussy bloomed, a low-grade tingle signaling her need for Saber. Normally, she enjoyed eating out at a restaurant, taking great delight in dissecting the various dishes on the menu. She liked to note the way the restaurateurs presented their dining room and meals.

Not tonight.

Tonight all she was aware of was Saber. They chatted about their time on the island and the various activities they could pursue and all the time they talked, Saber's hand caressed her shoulder, played with her hair or slipped under the table to stroke her leg.

The waitress brought their main courses. Earlier, she'd chosen fish, cooked two different ways. Emily thanked the waitress with a smile, almost jumping out of her skin when Saber ran his hand up her inner thigh and curled his fingers to check on the Ben Wa balls.

"Will there be anything else?" the waitress asked.

"No thanks," Saber said.

"Saber." Emily's voice held reprimand and she tried to wriggle away from his touch.

"You're turned-on."

"Of course I am," she whispered. "I want you to take out these wretched balls and put your cock there instead."

"Ah."

The laughter on his handsome face made her grin. She couldn't help it, despite her irritation. Actually, sexual frustration probably came closer to the truth. "This is your fault."

"If it makes you hot, then my wicked plan is working."

"Plan?"

"Yeah, kitten. Thanks to Leo's and Isabella's foresight, I have an excellent plan. Eat your dinner. You're going to need the energy."

Her channel flexed on hearing his words, gripping the Ben Wa balls. She stirred restlessly, her cheeks heating when she heard the faint tinkle of them.

Saber smirked. "Would you like to try my fish?" Before she could answer, he held a piece of the white flesh to her lips. "Open wide."

Fish wasn't exactly what she wanted to eat right now. Oh no. Right now she'd love to torture Saber, using her mouth on his cock until he begged for release. She'd take great delight in withholding his pleasure too. The wretched man.

Emily wasn't sure how she managed to get through her meal. She certainly couldn't describe the herbs and spices the chef had used during the cooking process. All she could think about was Saber thrusting deep inside her, driving them both to an incredible climax. She had difficulty withholding her groan of frustration as she grew progressively wetter.

"Would you like dessert or coffee?" the waitress asked as she collected their plates.

"No thank you," Emily said in a firm voice. She didn't want to give Saber the chance to delay a return to their room.

"That was great," Saber said. "We're fine."

Emily waited anxiously while the waitress brought their check for Saber to sign. Each time she moved a spike of pleasure zapped her. Judging by the gleam in her husband's sexy green eyes, he knew exactly what was going on. He signed the chit the waitress brought and stood. Emily's stomach lurched at the naughty grin twisting his lips. She held her breath and waited.

"You want me," he whispered, his breath a warm balm against her ear. "I can smell your arousal. Come on. Let's blow this joint." He took her hand in his and led her from the restaurant.

Emily walked gingerly as she wove past the tables, all too conscious of the jingle of the Ben Wa balls and the other diners who might hear the sound and jump to embarrassing conclusions.

Fiery torches lit the path leading to their *bure*. Emily's thighs brushed, the distinct dampness making her think she might explode if Saber didn't touch her soon.

"Did you enjoy your dinner?"

"I can hardly tell you what I ate," she retorted, scowling at him.

"I promised myself I wouldn't do this."

"Do what?" Her stomach pulled tight with sudden fear.

"This." Saber stepped off the path, yanking her after him. He rounded a tree and pulled her into the darkness cast by the shadows. Seconds later, he sank to his knees in front of her and lifted the midnight blue dress. Roughly, he nudged her legs apart and slipped his tongue over her damp folds. "God, you taste good."

The roughness of his tongue brought both relief and a desperate need for more. His tongue curled around her swollen clit then rasped across the sensitive nub. Once. Twice. Her orgasm exploded over her, a crashing series of waves as her pussy clamped down hard on the Ben Wa balls.

"Saber." She clutched his head and yanked his hair as the ripples in her vagina trailed off. Her breath came in choppy bursts. "God, Saber." Her fingers loosened the grip she had on his hair, and she caressed his cheeks, cupping his face when he glanced up at her.

"That's a reward for being so good tonight." He chuckled, the husky sound making her pulse skitter and desire pump through her again.

Emily grinned but rolled her eyes. "Every time you touched me during dinner I thought I'd expire on the spot. You know what they say about payback."

Saber didn't seem concerned, standing to fuse their mouths together. His arms wrapped around her, urging their bodies closer so she could feel his firm muscles and the bulge of his erection pressing against her softness. His fingers gripped her upper arms, holding her in place while he devoured her mouth.

Desire simmered in Emily again, a coil of energy in her lower body. She wriggled free, breathing harshly. "Let's go back to our room."

Without replying, Saber grasped her hand and dragged her back on the path. With tension pulsing between them, they made the ten-minute walk back to their *bure* in record time. Saber shouldered open the door and kicked off his shoes. Clothes and footwear flew in all directions, and soon they were both naked.

"On the bed," Saber ordered.

Emily didn't even think about refusing since that was what she wanted too. She wanted Saber to remove the Ben Wa balls and stuff her full of his cock. She reclined on the bed and gave in to the naughty impulse to touch herself. Half expecting Saber to growl a rebuke, she was surprised when he paused at the end of the bed to watch the show. His ridged abs flexed while his cock pulsed and, if anything, seemed to thicken. The teasing stroke around her clit faltered as she captured his gaze.

"Don't stop. I want you wet and ready for me because I intend to take you hard and fast."

"Tell me," she whispered hoarsely. "Describe how you're going to take me."

"Simple," Saber said. "I'm gonna tug out the Ben Wa balls, fit my cock to your entrance and enjoy the hot, wet slide as I enter you. I'm going to keep pushing into you until I'm balls-deep and can't go any farther."

Emily shivered as she imagined the mechanics and the sensations that would come hand-in-hand with Saber's possession. "Then what?"

"Then I'm gonna fuck you, kitten. I'm gonna invade your cunt with my cock until you're stuffed full with me.

I'll set a steady pace, retreating until you feel empty and crave me again. I'll soothe the ache until we both go up in sensual flames and explode with the pleasure."

"That sounds great." And it did. The ache he spoke of settled in her sex, the wet slide of her finger across her clit making the sensation deeper, her need more urgent. "Take me, Saber. Please."

"But I haven't told you what we're going to do at dinner tomorrow night."

The mischief she saw on his face reminded her of the expressions she saw on the twins' faces at times, or at least before Sly had gone to jail. Her smile faltered at the thought. But the truth—Saber might act like the leader of the feline community and speak sternly to his youngest brothers, but he exhibited some of their mischievous traits. Not that he'd agree if she mentioned it.

"Why don't you surprise me?" She sensed he wouldn't tell her anyway.

"I intend to." His green eyes glinted with hunger, and she watched him stroke his cock.

"Are you going to just talk, or are you going to take action? Sometime tonight."

"I need to ask you something first."

Emily's heart skipped a beat. Her finger ceased its comforting stroke across her clit. His voice hinted at something difficult he needed to ask her. Her mind whirred through the possibilities. She kept reminding herself he wouldn't want her sexually if he intended to leave her. The loving wouldn't feel so good, it wouldn't consume her so much if Saber wanted out. It's true they hadn't made love much since the loss of the baby, but since they'd arrived in Fiji, they'd started to make up for it. She and Michael hadn't had much sex before their final split. The sex they'd managed had been dreadful with no loving involved. Sex with Saber was different.

"What?" The word came out as an undignified croak. Fear replaced her previous arousal. She didn't know if she was ready for this, for whatever Saber wanted to say.

"Do you want me to use a condom?"

"What?" Emily gaped at him. His question wasn't the one she'd expected.

"A condom. Should I use one?"

Emily hesitated. She didn't think she could go through the pain of losing another child. Gavin had said she was healthy and there was no reason why she shouldn't carry a baby to full term. Logically she knew the miscarriage occurred because of an accident, but that didn't mean she'd conquered her fears. At the back of her mind lurked the feeling that she was defective and would never manage to give Saber a child. Yeah, she still worried he'd walk away because she couldn't give him what he wanted. Then there was the fact she might not even fall pregnant again. The first time had taken so long.

Swallowing, she glanced up at him. She saw concern, the frown between his brows hinting at worry. What she didn't see was anger or impatience. Emily took a deep breath and shook her head. "No, I don't think condoms are necessary."

"Good." That was all he said, but a beautiful smile lit his face, and suddenly Emily didn't fear the future quite as much.

Chapter Six

She didn't think condoms were necessary. Saber wanted to shout aloud and show the exuberant feelings bubbling through him. At least that meant she didn't intend to leave him. Just the thought of her departure filled him with apprehension, and he could almost feel the empty hole inside. He shivered and forced himself back to the present. To his mate, Emily.

Saber grasped the slippery string of the Ben Wa balls and pulled steadily. Emily moaned as the balls slowly emerged, glossy with her juices. Saber tossed the balls aside and settled in to taste his mate. He ran his tongue down her slit, his feline purring and rumbling beneath his skin. They both wanted this—to take Emily and make her scream with pleasure. His tongue scraped across her clit before retreating, her scent and taste filling him with pleasure. The only thing better would be filling her with his cock and feeling the subtle flex of her flesh caressing him. With tongue and fingers, he teased her until she trembled and pleaded for his possession.

"Saber, please do all those things you said you were going to do with me. Please." A sultry flush filled her face as she quivered under his ministrations.

"You have no idea how much I want that, kitten."

"Then what are you waiting for?"

"I'm waiting for you to concentrate on me." And she was. Right now he was the only thing filling her mind. It reminded him of better times and gave him hope for their future. Saber rose and guided his cock into her willing body. He sank into her clinging warmth with one hard stroke that made them both cry out. Then he set a hard pace, flinging them into pleasure and claiming her so she had no doubts as to who was fucking her and how he felt about her. He loved her—totally and absolutely.

Her fingernails dug into his shoulders, the sting of pain sending fierce need and clawing hunger through him. Saber licked her mark and she went crazy beneath him, groaning loudly, her channel squeezing him in rhythmic contractions. He pounded into her with a primal sense of satisfaction. This was what he'd wanted and needed—her utter surrender.

Saber plunged into his mate again and came in hard, almost painful spasms while Emily continued to cling to him. They drifted down from the orgasmic rush, their breathing in harmony. Aware he was probably crushing her, Saber pulled out and resettled beside her. Despite the balmy heat of the tropical evening, Emily crawled closer and wrapped her limbs around him.

Emotion, powerful and raw, rocked him then, and he had to squeeze his eyes closed to keep tears of joy at bay. It made him realize their relationship wasn't broken, merely bent, but fixable.

Silently, he thanked Gavin for the advice to go on holiday and Leo and Isabella for taking the time to buy their big brother sex toys, even if they'd really meant to embarrass him.

Tomorrow, he and Emily would talk about the baby, and this time he wouldn't tread warily. This time he'd tell the truth as he saw it, and he'd listen to Emily because what they had between them was magical.

It was worth fighting for.

EMILY STOOD AT THE wardrobe and wondered what she should wear today. Every muscle of her body ached, yet she hadn't felt so relaxed or at peace for ages.

Saber walked up behind her, still damp from the shower. He shut the wardrobe and grasped her hand in his, pulling her toward the front door of their *bure*.

"No clothes," he said firmly.

"But I'll get sunburned."

"We won't be outside for long, but you can take a sarong and suntan lotion."

Sweet mercy! Her heart did a distinct bump and grind on seeing the heat flashing in his eyes. Under normal circumstances she'd protest, but nothing about this holiday was ordinary. It was magical and seductive, and it gave her hope.

"I like looking at you." His smile lit up the entire *bure*.

"What about breakfast?" Her stomach gurgled to emphasize her point. After all the exercise, she needed to refuel. Funny, but today was the first time she'd felt like eating for ages. At mealtimes she forced herself to eat because she knew Saber or one of her sisters-in-law would comment if she didn't make the pretense. Emily grabbed her sarong and found a bottle of high-protection lotion to slather on once she hit the beach.

"I have breakfast covered." Saber snagged a small blue chiller bag before he led her outdoors.

Like the previous day, the sun was shining and the waves lapped at the shore. Out on the reef, larger waves crashed against the coral, kicking up a white wreath of churning water. The sand oozed between her toes and she sighed with contentment until she thought about their baby girl. Her satisfaction galloped away, replaced by remorse. She didn't deserve happiness. The moan of anguish she'd meant to keep to herself emerged as a pained croak. Saber shot her a sharp glance, the curl of his mouth flattening out to a scowl.

"Dammit, Emily. I hate the way you zone out on me." He stopped abruptly, dropped the chiller bag on the sand and turned to her with determination. Before she had time to blink, he'd spread her sarong on the sand and sat on it. "Come here." The icy tone of his voice did nothing to build her confidence.

Emily hesitated.

"Have I ever hurt you?"

"No."

"Then stop hovering like a mouse. I might be a feline but I can restrain myself."

Something in his face told her that while he wouldn't hurt her he had something else in mind. Before she could step closer, he sprang. He tackled her by the legs and had her over his knee before much more than a startled squeak escaped her. The flat of his hand stung when he applied it to her bare bottom. The second blow came quickly.

"I love you, dammit. I'm tired of you shutting me out. I'm tired of feeling as if I must tread on egg shells around you. I'm tired of hiding the way I feel. Don't you think I mourn for our daughter? Because, kitten, believe me, I've gone through all the emotions. The anger. The pleas and bargaining for things to be right again. You were in the wrong place at the wrong time. Losing our baby wasn't your fault."

Emily froze on hearing his impassioned words. She wriggled free of his touch and turned to face him.

Saber continued. "Losing our child wasn't my fault either. Do you think I don't wish I could change things? Hell yeah! I'd give my life in exchange for a different outcome. But I'm tired of you punishing me. I can't take it anymore."

Emily swallowed, mesmerized by the open passion on her mate's face. Saber normally kept his emotions contained. "Do you want to separate?"

His mouth dropped open a fraction, his teeth clacking when he snapped it shut. "Hell no," he barked. "Whatever gave you that idea? I love you. How many times do I have to tell you?"

Tears filled Emily's eyes. The stiffness left her body and she gave him a watery smile. "But I thought you blamed me. I thought you intended to walk away."

Saber moved then, grabbing her and hugging her so tight she feared for her ribs. He pressed desperate kisses to her face, her throat. Her mark. "Why the hell would you think that?"

"I kept thinking about Michael and how he rejected me. I...I thought it was happening again."

"Fuck, Emily." Saber grasped her upper arms and pulled back so he could see her expression. "I obviously need to spank you more often. The day your idiotic first husband left you was my gain. I'm not stupid enough to toss you away like yesterday's trash. I have never, ever considered my life without you in it."

"But you were so quiet after I lost our baby."

"I was grieving, kitten. I lost a child as well, except it was worse because I felt as if I lost my best friend and mate at the same time."

A tear overflowed and ran down her face. She gave him a watery smile. "Are we going to be all right now?"

"Do you love me?"

"More than anything." Emily ran her fingers across his cheek, the faint rasp of stubble sounding in the quiet that had fallen between them.

He grasped her hand and kissed her knuckles. "We still have lots of holiday in front of us. An isolated beach and a bag of sex toys."

Emily frowned. "But what if I can't have another baby?"

"I don't care. We can adopt or not have children at all. I love you. I don't mind as long as I can spend my life with you. God, that sounded sappy. Don't quote me to my brothers. They'll fall over themselves laughing."

Emily grinned. "From what I hear you have nothing to fear. Your brothers are quite romantic when they're in private with their mates."

Saber snorted but didn't ask questions. "I must have done something right then. Are we okay? About children, I mean."

"Maybe we could look into adoption when we get back? I've heard it takes a while or maybe we could foster kids."

"Either option would work for me. Do you want to go for a swim?"

"Is this a multi-choice quiz?" Emily smiled at the interest sparkling in Saber's eyes. She could almost hear him thinking.

"Yeah," he said slowly. "There is a plan B."

Her brows rose. "Yeah?"

Saber pounced. Emily found herself flat on her back with her mate leaning over her.

"I love you, Emily."

"So you keep saying. Isn't it time to show me?"

"As long as you promise me if you feel worried about our relationship at any time in the future you'll talk to me. Tell me what you're feeling so I can reassure you. If I do the same thing, then maybe we won't end up like this again."

"I promise."

"Good." Saber kissed her deeply, devouring her mouth and taking the mood from simmering to blazing hot in seconds flat. He played with her breasts, using hands and mouth to taunt and tease her. She shuddered at the fierce emotions that arced between them, aware of the damp readiness between her thighs. Each lingering touch was like a brand, the burn traveling deep. A sharp tug of her nipple sent a corresponding tug to her pussy.

"Saber, no more foreplay. I need you inside me now."

"I'm not gonna go easy on you, kitten. You need to be good and ready to take me."

Emily shivered at the thought of him using her hard. "I'm ready," she protested. "I feel like I might explode any second."

Saber paused. "On all fours. I want to go deep."

She scrambled to her hands and knees, glancing over her shoulder. The hard visage could have looked scary to anyone who didn't know him, but Emily didn't hesitate. She winked, a grin blooming. Slowly she wiggled her rump in a come-get-me sway.

The flat of his hand struck one buttock, making her jump. A second smack brought a groan along with a surge of pleasure. He'd never spanked her until this holiday, and she decided she liked it. She thought of the weeks ahead with pleasurable anticipation, positive there would be many more things to discover and experience with Saber. She hadn't had a chance to explore the bag Leo and Isabella had sent with Saber yet.

"Your arse looks pretty in pink."

"As long as it isn't sunburn."

"Not a chance," he said, covering her. Broad fingers stroked along her slit, delving shallowly. She pushed back, attempting to get a deeper penetration, but he just laughed, continuing to push her pleasure and frustration levels higher. Then finally, she felt him position his cock at her entrance. He thrust inside her with a masterful stroke that had them both groaning. He stretched her, driving in hard and deep. With each stroke, the exquisite tension inside her tightened until, finally, it snapped, tossing her into a world of acute pleasure. Her pussy grabbed at his cock, clutching the rigid shaft. He grunted, withdrew and pounded into her with several firm strokes before he stilled.

Emily could feel the strong beat of his heart, felt the surge of wetness in her sheath. He curled his larger body over her, murmuring words of love against her ear. Words she would never tire of. Despite the reason they were there, she was thankful they'd found each other again.

Saber pulled out of her and tugged her against his sweaty body. Their clammy flesh stuck together as they kissed.

"Come for a swim then we'll have breakfast." Saber tugged her to her feet and hand in hand they walked into the turquoise water.

"Are you going to give me a clue about what you have in mind for tonight?"

Saber chuckled, the rich sound bringing a rush of pleasure. He tapped her nose with his forefinger. "That's for me to know and you to find out."

"What exactly is in your sex toy bag of tricks?"

"Everything," Saber said dryly. "I'm glad they didn't decide to search it going through customs."

"So will I like this something?"

"Yes."

She didn't like the renewed glint in his green eyes. "Will it torture me?"

"Yes." His grin widened.

Emily sniffed. "I'm going to check out this bag before we go to dinner. Turnaround is fair play." She paused, allowing an imp of humor to fill her face. "I wonder if they have any cock rings."

And laughing at Saber's ragged intake of breath, she ran into the deeper water, full of confidence for the future. No matter what happened they'd face it together.

Bonus Chapter

Mitchell Farm, Middlemarch, New Zealand

Feline Shapeshifter Council Meeting.

Present: Sid Blackburn, Agnes Paisley, Valerie McClintock, Benjamin Urquart, London Allbright, Saber Mitchell

A thump on the front door announced the first of the council members to arrive for the meeting. Saber finished kissing Emily and loosened their embrace. He noted her rosy cheeks with satisfaction.

"I'm meant to be at the café," she said.

The oven timer went off and someone knocked on the front door again.

"I'll take the scones out of the oven and leave you in peace," Emily said.

"Kitten?"

"Yes?"

"I'll take care of dinner. Don't be late home 'cause I have plans." Saber waggled his brows and enjoyed seeing his mate's mouth fall open in nonplussed astonishment.

"Saber!" A querulous voice drifted through the closed door. "Are you going to let us in or not?"

"Better let in the hungry hordes," he said cheerfully and found himself whistling.

"What took you so long?" Agnes demanded.

"Emily and I were busy." Saber managed to maintain Agnes's gaze despite her loud *humph*. "We have cheese scones, hot from the oven."

Valerie rolled her eyes and followed her friend inside. "Ah, Emily. Good to see you looking so well. Both of you have a tan."

"It was a relaxing holiday," Emily said, her cheeks slipping from rosy into plain red and flustered. "Saber, I'll see you later."

Saber stared after his mate, his gaze lingering on her backside.

Agnes poked him in the belly. "Enough of that, young man."

"Ah, the others are here. Can we get this meeting underway? Saber, the tea and scones if you please," Valerie ordered.

Saber watched as Ben and Sid parked beside their vehicle, and London's old Mazda scuttled up the drive.

Chuckling, he wandered into the kitchen to sort out the tea. A few minutes later, London bustled in to help.

"The oldies are congratulating themselves on your good mood," she whispered as she picked up a tray bearing scones, jam and cream plus the milk jug. "Although I have to agree both you and Emily are looking heaps better." She paused in the doorway and winked. "Great tans."

"I think we'll be okay now," Saber said quietly. "I was worried for a while there."

London beamed. "I'm so pleased. If anyone deserves happiness it's you and Emily."

"Saber. London. What are you doing?" Valerie called. "We're waiting. We don't have all day."

Saber muttered a rude word and London giggled before they transported the tea things to the table in the other room, overlooking the garden. London poured the tea while Saber dispersed the scones.

Sid and Ben stopped their quiet talk and accepted their tea.

"You look better, lad," Sid said.

"Thank you. Have you had any trouble while I've been away?"

"It's been quiet. I think the residents were shocked at our hard stance," Sid replied.

Saber sipped his tea. "Good. I wasn't looking forward to playing the heavy."

"How is Sly?" Valerie asked.

London, bless her, glanced at his frozen expression and said, "We have a lot to discuss. Can we get started?" She tapped her pen on her notebook. "I'll begin. Plans for the Halloween house are coming along. Leo and Isabella are helping Joe set up the special effects in the house. All the other plans are in place for the children's events and the local businesses." London lifted her gaze to study them briefly before moving on to the next item. "I've drafted a plan for our shifter sighting drill." She handed a sheet of paper to each person and there was silence as everyone read the suggestions.

Saber glanced at them with approval. "This is perfect, London."

"Henry thinks the idea for big dogs is a good one, and he is willing to train them."

Saber stilled as an idea formed. "Do we have a source for dogs or puppies?"

"Henry has several contacts," London said. "And he'd like to do a home inspection to make sure the animals have the proper kenneling and care before a family adopts a dog."

"It's a clever idea," Ben commented. "We don't need a lot of big dogs around. Perhaps three or four. Just enough to cause an element of doubt if there is a problem sighting."

"I'm happy to liaise with Henry and London regarding the dogs. Now, for the rest of the plan. When do we want to do our drill?" Saber asked.

Agnes took a bite of her scone and swallowed before replying. "Let's present this plan as is at the next meeting and do our dry run the following weekend. We can have a drill every six months after that."

"Works for me," Sid said. "We can ask for volunteers to adopt the large dogs at the same time."

"The drill is an excellent idea," Valerie agreed. "I vote yes."

"Good," London said. "Now, we should probably think about Christmas. Now that we have more businesses in town, I suggest we have a Christmas parade. We can invite the neighboring towns and businesses to participate. We could also have a night of Christmas carols and perhaps a visit from Santa Claus with small presents for the children. The council could pay for the gifts since we have plenty of money in our account. And another thought, we could have a big Christmas tree near the school hall and turn on the lights at the beginning of the month. Maybe decorations for the street too."

Saber watched the oldies glance at each other and grin. He, too, was quietly impressed with London's efficiency and contribution to the council. "That is the perfect way to end the year. Good thinking, London."

"We'll take care of the Christmas plans," Agnes said and the other oldies nodded with enthusiasm. "We'll let you know our plan of attack at the next meeting."

"Fine with me," Saber said.

"Me, too." London closed her notebook. "That's everything."

"Excellent. Thank you, Saber. London." Valerie rose. "I must get home. We have visitors coming for dinner. You ready, Agnes?"

Saber showed the oldies out and when he returned he found London had cleared the table for him. "Thanks."

"No problem." She pushed out a hard breath. "I always feel in need of a glass of wine after one of these meetings."

Saber barked out a laugh. "They do have a way of driving one to drink. Do you know if Henry is at home? I'd like to speak to him about the dogs."

"Yes, he's working from home today. Do you want to come with me now? You could have a beer while I have a glass of wine."

Saber grinned. "Deal. I'll be there in ten minutes."

Later that evening, he arranged dinner. Pizza and salad. Nothing special, but he knew Emily appreciated not having to cook after working for most of the day.

He heard Emily's car and went to meet her at the front door. "Kitten, I missed you." He kissed her, trapping her reply with his lips, but he didn't think she minded because her arms curled around his neck, drawing him closer.

They were both breathing hard when they pulled apart.

"I've got pizza and salad for dinner. Would you like a glass of wine?"

"I'd love one," Emily said. "Do I have time for a quick shower?"

"Ten minutes," Saber warned, a wave of love engulfing him as he studied his mate.

"What about my surprise?"

He couldn't resist stroking her hair, now glossy with golden highlights. "During and after dinner."

"Do I get a clue?"

"No." He slapped her on the backside to hurry her along. "Ten minutes. Dress casual."

Her brown eyes widened and his delight in her reaction zapped all the way to his cock.

Emily arrived back in the kitchen in eight minutes, wearing her ruby-red robe and her feet bare. Saber smiled at the red polish on her toenails. It was a relief to feel back in step with his mate again.

"My surprise?" she prompted.

Saber handed her a glass of red wine and ushered her to the dining room. Two candles offered illumination while the scent of freesias perfumed the air since he'd taken the time to pick a bunch.

"Oh, Saber." Emily sent him a misty smile.

The oven timer dinged. "Wait there while I get the pizza."

He cut the pizza and toted it into the dining room before darting back to get the salad. Finally, he dropped into the seat opposite her.

"This looks delicious."

"It's not much, but I wanted to spoil you and show you how happy I am that you're my mate. No matter what happens in the future, whether we have children or not, I want you to know that I love you. I will always love you."

"Oh Saber." This time a tear trickled free but he sensed it was still a happy occasion.

"As part of our plan to keep our community safe, several families will be adopting large breed dogs. How do you feel about having a puppy? Henry has friends who have a litter of puppies. They're looking for good homes for them, and Henry said he'd help us train our dog if we decided to get one."

Emily nodded immediately, and Saber's heart flip-flopped against his ribs at her joy, her happiness. "I'd love a puppy."

"Henry said he'd take us this weekend if we were interested."

"Yes." Emily bounced on her seat. "That is an awesome surprise. Thank you!"

"A puppy isn't my surprise."

"No?"

"No. How would you feel about having dessert in bed?"

"What's for dessert?"

Saber smiled and reached across the table for her hand. "Early season strawberries and chocolate dip."

"That sounds doable," she agreed, a twinkle in her eyes.

"Well, eat your pizza otherwise there won't be any dessert for you."

Emily chuckled, a saucy, sassy gurgle that had Saber's smile broadening.

His mate was back.

His Emily.

He stood and held out his hand. "I've had enough pizza for now. How about you?"

Her fingers curled around his, and she stood. Yes, his Emily was back, and whatever trials or tribulations rained down on them, they would weather them as a team.

Emily and Saber Mitchell—together forever.

THANK YOU FOR READING *My Blue Lady*. I hope you enjoyed spending time with Emily and Saber. I bet you want to know what's up with Sly and jail, right? Well, I can give you a hint and tell you that Sly and Joe, the Mitchell twins, meet a new Middlemarch arrival and their story, *My Twin Trouble*, is out now.

The best way to keep up with new releases is to join my newsletter (www.shelleymunro.com/newsletter) or to follow me on Bookbub (www.bookbub.com/authors/shelley-munro), so you receive release notifications.

Please turn the page to read an excerpt from *MY TWIN TROUBLE* plus an excerpt from *SNARED BY SABER*, the first book in the spinoff series, Middlemarch Capture.

EXCERPT — MY TWIN TROUBLE

"SOMEONE PURCHASED THE GARAGE in town."

The mischief in his twin brother snared Sly Mitchell's attention seconds after Joe burst into the kitchen of their newly purchased Middlemarch farmhouse. He recognized the glee in his brother. A punch line lurked somewhere, waiting to pounce at him.

Joe tossed the latest issue of the *New Zealand Times* newspaper and the day's mail on the kitchen counter. A bunch of keys clattered as they landed inside an empty fruit bowl. "A woman."

A chuckle burst from Sly. "You're kidding."

"Does this face look as if it's joking?" Joe paused a beat, amusement tilting up the corners of his mouth. "A single woman."

"Okay, what's the joke? You might as well tell me everything. She looks like the back end of a bus. She has warts on the end of her nose. She's fifty-plus with wrinkles."

"Not from where I was standing. She's a babe. Curvy. Vivacious." Joe winked at him. "Shifter."

"Yeah?"

"Around our age. I liked her."

Interest stirred in Sly. He and Joe were identical twins. They looked alike with their short, black hair and green eyes. Sexy, according to his sisters-in-law and the women they met. They enjoyed the same things and bore an uncanny ability to determine what the other had on his mind. Their family suspected telepathy, but they didn't communicate via mind. It was more an instinctive understanding of the way they both saw the world. Joe wasn't like him. He was *him*.

Sly picked up the mail and flicked through the bills before tossing them aside. "I thought we'd decided to woo Maggie to our way of thinking." He snatched up the newspaper and ripped off the outer plastic covering, absently unfolding the pages while he frowned at Joe.

"Did I say anything about commitment? Kiera Pascoe is about fun. She's not interested in anything serious either."

"You guys must've enjoyed an intense chat." Sly flicked through the paper, scanning the pages for items of interest.

"Not really, but we hit—"

"What the fuck?" Sly interrupted, staring at a small article in the social section.

Joe stood beside him in seconds. "What is it? What's wrong?"

"This." Sly slammed his fist on top of the table. "How could she? We had an understanding."

"Maggie?" Joe shoved his brother aside. "If you move your hand, I might have a hope of reading the bloody article."

"I'll read the notice for you. *Catherine Scarlet of Dunedin is delighted to announce the engagement of her only daughter Margaret Judith to Nathaniel Henry Charles, eldest son of Henry and Elizabeth Napier of Dunedin.* Maggie's fuckin' engaged."

"When? Does the paper say when she's getting married?"

"No mention of a date." Sly scowled and started to pace. "We need to talk to her or, better yet, spend a few days with her. Alone."

It was Joe's turn to frown. Although he liked Maggie and they'd had some fun times together, he didn't feel the same way about her as his brother. The lack of connection troubled him. He should tell Sly the truth yet he'd hesitated. There was something about Maggie that put him on guard. It was difficult to explain to himself let alone to his brother.

"We'll go and visit her." Sly grabbed the car keys from the fruit bowl. "Tonight."

"How about a shower before we drive to Dunedin? I'm covered in mud." His nostrils flared when he inhaled. "And you have the distinct whiff of cow shit."

Sly sniffed loudly, his nose wrinkling in a feline manner. "Good point. We'll leave in half an hour."

Twilight gave way to evening by the time they pulled up outside the two-bedroom house Maggie shared with one of her friends in an expensive suburb of Dunedin. Sly jumped out of their mud-splattered SUV and hurried to the front door while Joe followed at a slower pace.

They hadn't seen Maggie recently, mainly because they'd been busy with their newly purchased farm. Perhaps catching up with her wouldn't hurt. Despite Joe's unspoken qualms, the three of them enjoyed a dynamite time together in bed.

The door opened and Maggie stared out at them. The last time they'd seen her she'd sported unruly brown hair. Now her curly hair lay sleek against her skull. The golden highlights added another layer of sophistication as did the makeup and the black dress skimming her slimmed-down curves.

"Maggie." Sly took possession of her right hand and kissed the back. "You look gorgeous."

"Sly. Joe." She glanced down the footpath before opening the door fully. "Come in. It's great to see you both. I was ready to shout at my roomie for losing her key again."

They both stepped inside and waited for Maggie to close the door after them. The instant the door shut, Sly grabbed Maggie for a passionate kiss. Her arms wound around his neck and she pressed her lithe body against him.

Her exotic spicy scent filled Joe's senses and hauled him in like a trout. Unable to help himself, he tapped Sly on the shoulder. "Can I have a turn?"

Laughing, his face blazing full of happiness, Sly stepped back to let Joe take his place with Maggie. Maggie's brown eyes glittered with an expression Joe couldn't read, then her soft lips met his and the fleeting worry faded from his mind. She trembled in his arms and a spear of sheer lust filled him. They'd worked hard lately, racking up long hours to get their farm into production. These days, a drink out at the local Middlemarch pub with Jonno, Jake and Hari was about their limit.

Aware of the questions they needed to ask before they carried Maggie off to their bed, Joe released her. "I understand you're engaged."

Maggie let out a derisive snort, a surprising tone that didn't tally with her current feminine image. "My mother likes Nathaniel. Come into the kitchen while I get some drinks."

"She should marry him," Sly said, following. "We had an understanding."

"He wore me down." Maggie reached into the fridge for two beers. She placed them on the counter and grabbed an open bottle of white wine. "The second I wavered, he pushed a ring on my finger."

"Why didn't you contact us?" Sly asked.

Joe remained quiet. While Maggie seemed pleased they'd turned up, something didn't jibe with her behavior. He sank onto a barstool and watched her closely while she fussed with drinks.

"I'm not sure if I can live in Middlemarch."

Joe inclined his head. At least she admitted her misgivings.

"Don't tell me you're frightened of Emily?" Sly made a scoffing noise. "Joe and I have our own place now and six hundred acres. Come and visit. Spend the weekend."

"I'm meant to go out with friends tomorrow."

"Blow them off." Sly radiated calm confidence. "Come on. You want to spend the weekend with us."

Joe started to object, intending to tell his brother he didn't agree with his plan. A quick glance at Maggie changed his mind. A brittle edge framed her smile as if she forced her happiness to the surface. Maybe he needed to stand back and let the truth unfold for Sly. That way, Sly couldn't pine after something that wasn't right at a later date.

Strangely disconnected from their meeting, Joe continued to study her closely. The large diamond weighed down her finger in an almost obscene display of disposable income. This Nathaniel possessed big-time money and prestige while he and Sly owned six hundred acres and a mortgage. Sure, Saber would have lent them money if they'd requested a loan. Probably Leo and Felix would've chipped in too. They hadn't approached their brothers because they'd wanted to do everything on their own rather than rely on family connections.

Maggie knew nothing of their feline nature either, and Joe couldn't envisage telling her—another fact to worry him. While they'd spent some fun times together, Maggie tended to treat them like a convenience. She let them have her body and time when it suited her.

He saw the problems with their relationship. Why couldn't Sly?

Read **My Twin Trouble** today.

(www.shelleymunro.com/books/my-twin-trouble)

EXCERPT — SNARED BY SABER

JUMP INTO THE FUTURE when the descendants of our Middlemarch Shifters make a new life in another world...

"What do you think?" Saber Mitchell studied his four brothers, who were currently crowding his office, two sprawled in chairs and the other two leaning against the walls. He scanned each of his brothers' faces before focusing on Felix, the second oldest of the Mitchell brothers. Leo came next in age, followed by the twins Sly and Joe. They had one more sibling, their sister Scarlett, who was the youngest of the Mitchell clan.

"I still think this is a crazy idea," Leo said. "Why can't we focus on farming the land? We had a successful farm on Earth. There's no reason we can't replicate that again."

"We don't need mates," Felix said, folding his arms across his chest. His green eyes—the same green eyes Saber saw in his bedroom mirror each day—offered a dare.

"They won't necessarily keep us on the straight and narrow," troublemaker Joe agreed. "Women are good for one thing."

"Your Mission Mate plan is flawed," Sly said, with a smirk at his twin. "Ma might think copying an idea our ancestors used successfully will fix everything, but it won't. I don't want to settle with one woman. Leo is right. We should focus on the land. If we're dog-tired we won't have time or energy for fucking around."

Saber fought the urge to knock his brothers' heads together. No point wasting the energy. Violence wouldn't dent their heads or their confidence. Ever since they'd left Earth with a large contingent of friends and family to escape the feline virus, trouble had followed them. Often expensive trouble, with his brothers as the ringleaders.

"We don't have the luxury of waiting for the land to become productive." Saber strove for calm and logical arguments. "We have to take the assets we possess and use them to support our group. That means making the resort a success—and finding mates before the males kill each other."

"What about the zylon? Their numbers are increasing again. If they get through the protective fencing and into the resort, we'll have dead guests," Leo said. "Excellent publicity for Middlemarch Resort. It was lucky I grabbed that zylon this morning before the woman tried to stroke the bloody thing."

Saber failed to repress a shudder when he thought of the possible headlines that could race to Dalcon, their largest market so far. *Guests at Exclusive Middlemarch Resort Die from Zylon Bites.*

He couldn't let that happen.

"We'll go hunting tonight after the welcome party," Saber said, wishing he knew what was up with Leo. His normally even-tempered brother had become moody. He'd been acting weirdly since they'd left Dalcon. Maybe Ma knew. He'd ask at the next opportunity.

Saber drummed his fingers on the top of his desk. "You've all wandered through the foyer during check-in.

Did any of the women catch your eye? Did you spot possibles for the first captures?"

"I went through the booking forms again last night. On paper, the two females in chalet twenty-five look good," Felix said. "From what Scarlett dug up during her comp research, they have little or limited interaction with family. We could capture one of them."

"That was the two females Leo and I saw with the zylon," Saber said. "Did they book together? Do they know each other?"

"Scarlett said one of them booked on behalf of the other. I want a visual before I agree to go ahead. I'll deliver their luggage," Felix said and stood to leave. "If we don't like them after the capture, we can change our minds, right? They don't need to know the capture might become permanent?"

"You can change your mind if you don't gel with your capture." Saber hoped like hell that wouldn't happen. "Leo, you should check them out again too. Help Felix with the delivery."

Leo muttered under his breath but pushed away from the wall and stomped after Felix.

"What's up with Leo?" Joe asked.

"I was hoping you knew," Saber said.

"We know nothing." Sly shot a mischievous glance at his twin. "Do you need us to do anything? I've got animals to feed and the irrigation system is playing up again."

"No, that's fine. Just make sure you don't miss the welcome party," Saber warned. "And if the zylon population is increasing again, we need you both on the hunt tonight."

Joe flashed a cheeky grin and saluted. "Aye-aye, bro."

"We wouldn't miss the opening party for Mission Capture," Sly said, his expression a replica of his twin's—impudent.

Saber snorted and waved them out. He'd planned and schemed and lied to get to this point. The captures would work. They had to because he'd run out of options.

A tap sounded on his door and he straightened from his slump. "Yeah?"

The door opened and his mother, Anna Mitchell, walked in. She took a seat in front of his desk. "Everything set for the welcome reception? Can I do anything to help?"

His mother was tall and slender, her black hair long and without a hint of gray. She was the sole Mitchell without green eyes. He and his siblings took after their father in appearance. A widow of five years, his mother surprised most people when they learned she had six adult offspring.

"No, Ma. We've planned for every possible contingency. I just pray this crazy plan works."

"It worked for our ancestors," she said, her gray eyes flinty with determination. "The original Saber Mitchell met Emily Scarlett at the first Middlemarch dance in New Zealand."

"But we intend to keep the women against their will. I don't think our ancestors went to that extreme."

Anna made a scoffing sound. "Females enjoy a man who takes control, one who protects them and makes them feel feminine. Every guest at the resort is dying to use the capture-fantasy room. Many of them fantasize about forced sex. We're providing a legitimate service, and the women who are chosen will be lucky to secure one of my gorgeous sons in return." She reached over and patted his hand. "Don't worry, son. Everything will work out for the best. It did for our ancestors. You only have to read Emily's diaries to know how happy she and Saber were together."

Saber prayed his mother was right. "Did Scarlett finish researching the Tigrus race? I want to know how compatible they'd be with us."

"She said she sent the last of the information you requested to your private mini-tab."

"Thanks."

Anna stood and glided to the door. "I'm going to mingle with the women and check everything is going smoothly."

Once again Saber stared at the closed door and hoped like hell this crazy plan went the way they hoped.

He slumped in his chair, exhausted—both mentally and physically. Tired of fighting for survival. Tired of looking after their people.

Just tired.

The welcome party was in full swing when Saber walked into the function room flanked by his brothers. His nostrils flared, quivered at the scent of lust thick on the air. His stride faltered as the wave hit him, reminded him he was a healthy feline male who hadn't had a woman for months.

Felix gave a soft whistle while Leo cursed under his breath.

"Everyone seems happy," Joe said in patent understatement. "Even Laurence is smiling for a change."

Music played and several females were dancing with employees. Laughter and excited chatter battled the music, and some of the tension lifted from Saber's shoulders. Everyone looked happy. In fact, all the men they employed were talking or dancing with their guests. Doing their job, including Laurence, the brother of Saber's dead fiancée, which marked a change.

Taking care to keep his breaths shallow Saber said in a low voice, "Go and check out the women on our list. Dance with them, speak with them and come to a decision. We need to cement our plans."

As his brothers wandered off, Saber observed the partygoers. A flash of red caught his attention, and he turned to watch a woman progress to the bar. She wasn't exceptionally beautiful like some of the other women and was on the skinny side, yet something undefinable kept his gaze stitched in place. The red gown followed the lines of her body, its short length showcasing her legs and cupping her backside. Her footwear consisted of a series of crisscrossed black straps and heels that elevated her height. She chatted with the bar staff, shared a smile with the other women who sat at the bar and politely turned down a request to dance.

Interesting. He hadn't noticed any other woman saying no. Most were here to enjoy themselves and interact with the men.

Saber stalked closer, his mind taking in the small details and matching them against his brothers' tastes. Honey-blonde hair, swept into some complicated style that made a man think about messing it up. A slight, petite frame. Bright blue eyes the color of the cornflowers his mother used to grow swept over him, dismissed him without pause.

Saber felt his mouth drop open and snapped it shut. Her rejection rankled. Miffed, he took a step toward her before common sense reasserted itself.

He wanted mates for his brothers.

He wanted them settled.

Happy.

This was business, and his own physical needs weren't paramount.

Saber changed direction and hit the far end of the bar. He signaled for a drink and turned to survey the room before his gaze tracked back to the woman. Another female joined Blondie. Tall and regal with ruthlessly short black hair, she was dressed in a deep-blue dress with a dramatic slit up one side.

His attention shifted back to Blondie—just in time to see Felix swoop. Minutes later, Leo joined them and started chatting with the friend.

Saber watched for a few seconds longer, batted back the surge of inappropriate resentment and decided everything was going well. He wasn't needed. His brothers knew what to do, and for once they were following orders. He downed his drink and stopped to chat now and then, pulling out his rusty social skills to flirt and drag responding smiles from their female guests. Some of the women were stunning beauties, others not so much, yet their smiles and excitement, their enjoyment, made them all rate a second inspection.

He wove through the guests and employees, the lustful scents starting to get to him.

"Saber." His sister Scarlett waved him over to where she was sitting by the terrace doors.

He dropped onto a seat beside her. "What are you doing here?"

"I wanted to check out the guests, get a feeling for them." She delicately sniffed the air and grimaced. "Sucks to be a shifter sometimes." Her gaze drilled into him. "I didn't get to spend long on reception because you had me running background checks all day." She leaned closer, lowering her voice a fraction. "One of the women in chalet twenty-five doesn't have any family, although there was some scandal about her accusing her in-laws of murdering her husband. Nothing came of her allegations, and I haven't been able to discover anything recent on the subject."

"Pity we don't have time to visit her residence and ask questions in person. I worry we'll miss something important," Saber said. "What about the other one?"

"She comes from a military background, although sources say she doesn't spend her leave with her family. She seems closer to an aunt—her mother's sister. If we grabbed her, the military might become involved. The woman with no family might make things easier."

Saber tapped his fingers on his thigh. "True. Or maybe we should scoop up both women. If they both disappeared we'd have some breathing space, rather than leaving one behind who might cause problems and raise the alarm."

"Good point," Scarlett said. "We're treading a delicate line with our capture plan."

Low, throaty laughter came from a neighboring couple. It was sexy and suggestive and the insinuation transmitted with ease. The resort employee stood and held out his hand to the woman, a Dalcon local, Saber thought.

"Care for a walk along the beach?" the man asked.

The laughter was a purr of response this time as she accepted his hand and stood.

Saber shot a glance at his sister. "You shouldn't be here, Scarlett. It's not right."

Scarlett reached over and rapped her fist against his skull. "Hello? Hello? Is anybody there?"

Saber ducked out of reach. "Cut it out."

"Then stop treating me like a kid. I know what sex is, Saber."

"Who told you about sex? Tell me so I can shoot their kneecaps."

"Saber!"

Saber grinned, silently acknowledging his sister was an adult. She wasn't a cute kid tagging after him anymore. "We're going hunting for zylon once this winds down. You wanna come?"

"You're on. Bet I catch more cute fluffies than you."

"You can try," Saber said.

Romantic cooing sounded outside and Scarlett grimaced. "Ugh, I've seen enough. I'll see you later." She stood and sashayed out the terrace doors. She paused to remove her shoes before stepping onto the sandy beach.

Saber watched his sister until she blended with the darkness. They had a couple of days to observe and decide. Maybe this capture scenario was bizarre and risky, but he was doing it for his family. Once they were settled the burden of responsibility would lessen, and he wouldn't need to worry as much about his family's future. He could relax.

Read **Snared by Saber** today.

(www.shelleymunro.com/books/snared-by-saber)

ABOUT AUTHOR

USA Today bestselling author Shelley Munro lives in Auckland, the City of Sails, with her husband and a cheeky Jack Russell/mystery breed dog.

Typical New Zealanders, Shelley and her husband left home for their big OE soon after they married (translation of New Zealand speak - big overseas experience). A twelve-month-long adventure lengthened to six years of roaming the world. Enduring memories include being almost sat on by a mountain gorilla in Rwanda, lazing on white sandy beaches in India, whale watching in Alaska, searching for leprechauns in Ireland, and dealing with ghosts in an English pub.

While travel is still a big attraction, these days Shelley is most likely found in front of her computer following another love - that of writing stories of contemporary and paranormal romance and adventure. Other interests include watching rugby (strictly for research purposes), cycling, playing croquet and the ukelele, and curling up with an enjoyable book.

Visit Shelley at her Website
www.shelleymunro.com

Join Shelley's Newsletter
www.shelleymunro.com/newsletter

Also By Shelley

Paranormal

Middlemarch Shifters

My Scarlet Woman

My Younger Lover

My Peeping Tom

My Assassin

My Estranged Lover

My Feline Protector

My Determined Suitor

My Cat Burglar

My Stray Cat

My Second Chance

My Plan B

My Cat Nap

My Romantic Tangle

My Blue Lady

My Twin Trouble

My Precious Gift

Middlemarch Gathering

My Highland Mate

My Highland Fling

Middlemarch Capture

Snared by Saber

Favored by Felix

Lost with Leo

Spellbound with Sly

Journey with Joe

Star-Crossed with Scarlett